Single in Southeast Texas

Single in Southeast Texas

by

Gretchen Johnson

Golden Antelope Press
715 E. McPherson
Kirksville, Missouri 63501
2017

ISBN   978-1-936135-32-5 (1-936135-32-9)

Library of Congress Control Number: 2017945504

Published by:
Golden Antelope Press
715 E. McPherson
Kirksville, Missouri 63501

Available at:
Golden Antelope Press
715 E. McPherson
Kirksville, Missouri, 63501
Phone: (660) 665-0273
http://www.goldenantelope.com
Email: ndelmoni@gmail.com

For my husband, Tom Sowers,
the man who taught me that Southeast Texas
can be the most romantic place on earth.

Acknowledgments:

I'd like to thank Betsy and Neal Delmonico for all their help with the book and for the guidance to alter the original draft and make it something stronger.

I'm eternally grateful to my family – Brian and Lois Johnson, Alex, Jes, Emmett, Paige, and Brooks – and to my dearest friend, Jenni Nelmark.

Thanks to the Lamar University English Department for bringing me to Beaumont and for helping me to see the beauty in this place.

And thanks to Kimberly Pehrson for all the support while I was writing this book.

Contents

Chapter One: Beaumont

The year after I moved to Beaumont, Texas, Hurricane Humberto visited in the middle of the night. Many of the city's residents slept right through, not impressed enough by a category one storm to be pulled out of their beds at three a.m. But when the branches whipped against my windows and the immense swirling whirr of the wind circled the brick walls of my apartment building, I awoke quickly, got out of bed, stood still for a moment with wide open eyes, and went out to the living room to watch the storm through the patio window.

Around four, the wind and rain stopped, and an intense calm settled in the night sky. Suddenly I longed to be out in it, to feel the atmosphere after the storm. I put on shoes and shorts and raced downstairs. I ran outside and splashed through the puddles on pavement and toward the middle of the lot to inhale the stillness.

"We're in the eye, you know?" a man's voice yelled from across the lot.

"The what?" I yelled back, walking toward him.

"The eye ... the eye of the hurricane. I've never seen this before. My girlfriend ... she's sleeping," he said, waving his arms wildly. "Hurricanes ain't nothin' to her. She's lived down here her whole life, but I've never seen this before. We're right in the middle of it. Can you believe it? I had to feel this, to be out in it. You never know when you'll get a chance like this again."

"So it isn't over yet?" I asked.

"Oh, no. We're standing right in the middle of the storm, right in the middle of a hurricane. Everyone else is sleeping, but here we are. I can't freakin' believe it."

"Yeah, it's pretty amazing."

"Just don't stay out here too long. You don't want to be out here when the other side of this thing hits," he said.

"I won't," I said, and we both stood silent for a moment, strangers connected by the fleeting pleasure of hesitation, before he nodded his goodbye, walked past me and back into the building behind us. For a few minutes I just stood there, staring straight into the calm hum of the eye of Hurricane Humberto as Beaumont slept peacefully for a few more breaths.

*

The year before, in 2006, my life sustained its own hurricane force winds. After only two years of marriage, my husband Blake had an affair with a nineteen-year-old he met at work. I had just finished graduate school in San Marcos, had just interviewed for the teaching job I would later be offered in Beaumont, had just decided to stop taking birth control pills, and then everything changed. Just as Hurricane Humberto surprised coastal inhabitants by intensifying from a tropical storm to a hurricane right before landfall, my own disaster caught me unprepared.

I was twenty-six and living under the false assumption that something like infidelity happened in someone else's life, not my own. Blake had moved with me from Minnesota to Texas when I started my master's degree, a display of loyalty that lured me into believing it was impossible that his commitment could ever falter. Of course, looking back on it all, the signs were there from the start – the habitual lying about finances, the fascination with John Mayer and Charlie Sheen, the inability to follow through on projects, and the always-changing list of loyal and attractive female friends – but it's hard to see the storms up ahead when tranquil spring days seem to stretch out endlessly before us.

After I found out about the affair, it was hard to know what to do, so for a while, I did nothing. With all the emotional debris scattered across my mind, I made my way through days numb to my own circumstances. Blake's blue eyes, strawberry hair, and deep voice still sang to my senses as they had before, but I hated him. The affair-girl, having only spent two months in town to visit her cousin, had moved on, but my pain stayed right there.

I looked around our tiny apartment, studied all the framed photos of Blake and me, repeatedly read the cards and letters we had exchanged, and analyzed the parade of presents we had given one another. While Blake was at work, I made little piles of these items, artifacts of our relationship spread out on the surfaces of our apartment. I was looking for an answer, searching desperately for the exact moment the storm winds began to stir, but I couldn't find anything. There were no answers.

*

At the end of that summer, Blake and I moved to Beaumont, a town I had never even heard of when I first saw the job posting, a town of about 100,000 people, which I would later learn was known for its high STD and crime rates and for being frequently cited in studies of America's worst cities to call home, a town that was only beginning to recover from the devastating effects of Hurricane Rita, a town still stuck in the shadows of racial tension. I knew my marriage wasn't going to work out, but it took two more months for me to say it.

The day I signed my lease, the apartment manager handed me my keys, smiled, and said, "This is a really nice part of town. You'll like it. It's mostly white."

There I was – soon to be single again and an outsider in a place I didn't understand.

At work, I smiled too much, exerted myself in classes and conversations with overt enthusiasm. An older colleague stopped me in the hallway one afternoon and said, "What are you so damn happy about? Don't you know where you're living? This is Beaumont, Texas. Where the hell do you think you are?"

Stunned and confused, I stuttered, "I'm ... I'm ... well ... I guess I'm just so happy to have a job ... this job. I mean, I really like teaching here, not *here* the town ... *here* the school." I felt like an idiot as she walked off, gray head shaking, and shut her office door behind her. She didn't know that behind my smile I was walking wounded through the dark avenues of days, that under my clothes the deep lacerations of lost love stung and bled beneath the scarred skin, that the new job was helping to heal me.

My older colleague was right, though. I didn't know Beaumont yet. Even my own language sounded different there. I struggled to decipher the thick Cajun accents many of my students had, sometimes asking them to repeat a phrase several times before finally getting it. The day before fall classes began, a student came to my office to ask a question and introduced himself as "Rauls."

"Rauls?" I asked.

"No, Rauls," he repeated, but it sounded the same to me.

"Rauls?" I asked, taking another stab at it.

"No, it's Rauls," he said again but slower and louder.

"Oh, okay. Nice to meet you," I said, giving up. When the class rolls came in the next day, I figured it out. His name was Russ.

The old-fashioned culture of the region often upset and confused me, leaving me disillusioned with my own religion after standing up for the third time, right in the middle of a sermon, to venture outside and away from a pastor preaching hatred of Middle Eastern people or homosexuality. I sat in coffee shops and listened to women's bible groups reassure each other that a woman's duty is to stay silent in church and to obey her husband's every demand at home.

I drove to work through a landscape of yards scattered with trash, noticed barely inhabitable houses with old cars parked out front, and wondered who bought groceries at the dirty roadside stands I passed. There was something beautiful about it, though, something more real than San Marcos or the suburb I grew up in back in Minnesota, and even though I was often uncomfortable in my new city, I wanted to be there.

Slowly I started to understand what it meant to live in Beaumont, Texas. It meant living with the constant reminder of poverty and the yearly threat of hurricanes. It meant searching for beauty in old and abandoned buildings. It meant the ability to see structures for what they once were and to accept their unrepaired state with a reverence for the real, the ability to stare deeply enough into an old house to recover its soul. Living in Beaumont meant turning the music up a little louder, looking at people for who they were and not always for what they were saying. It meant letting go of my old dreams, the ones where Blake's love could light up even the corridors behind closed eyes, like the familiar glow that fills an afternoon during a long sun-shower. It meant understanding that Blake would never walk through my door again, that I would never hear his new stories, feel his strong hands on my skin, or stay up late with him making tacos and dancing without music in our old apartment. And it meant knowing that maybe, standing there in the middle of my greatest disappointment, I would somehow find my life again.

Chapter Two: Damien

A year after Blake moved out, the bar of soap he left in the shower still sat there, a square green reminder of what my life used to be. I couldn't get myself to throw it away or let it dissolve quickly in the drain, but the soap cradle sat just below the shower head, that place where steamy mist softens soap and slowly weakens its constitution. A few months after Blake left, I started to notice the bar getting smaller. It was sinking slowly into the soap grate, causing tiny fragments to fall to the drain, leaving the square a little smaller with each shower.

As I finished my shower that day, I noticed that only a few soap shreds remained, and I knew that soon the soap would be completely gone.

It was Saturday again, and I had slept until two again, leaving myself only a few hours of daylight and little motivation to even leave my apartment. I dressed quickly, pulled my hair into a bun, and made myself a peanut butter and honey sandwich.

Novembers in Beaumont were still warm, so I ate with the windows open and could almost feel the pulse of people in cities far away as the humid gulf breezes sailed through my apartment. For a moment, I loved the idea of solitude and reminded myself of the pleasure of an afternoon in Paris when I listened to strangers discuss politics in a language I didn't know as I settled inward to my own thoughts. I thought too of the few moments in my life where I stood in the middle of the purest kind of human connec-

7

tion and realized that, even in those moments, we always remain separated by the secret tunnels of our own minds.

*

Around four, I started feeling restless and decided to head to Wuthering Heights Park for a walk. Unlike cities like Minneapolis and Seattle, Beaumont offered few options for outdoor recreation. Wuthering Heights Park, a half-mile loop of tree-lined walkways, was one of only a few local parks and served as a welcome respite from a region where swamps replaced lakes and strip clubs stood on the same streets as schools.

The park was fairly empty as usual, a fact that had surprised me on my first few visits since it was one of the few scenic spots in town. Fall was in full bloom, but it was different than a northern fall. In southern Texas, the leaves changed from their summer greens to muted oranges and yellows but never shifted over into the spectrum of intense autumn shades, and trees only shed some of their leaves, as though they knew that winter was never really coming.

As the first snow storm swirled over my Minnesota hometown, I luxuriated in the feeling of a seventy degree atmosphere. I watched a woman with three dachshunds walk so quickly that the little dogs had to sprint at a desperate pace just to keep up, and I heard a frustrated couple argue on a park bench as I passed by.

It felt good to be out of my apartment, to be seen by strangers and breathe in the fall foliage. I thought about all the places I had been and decided that Beaumont's towering trees, the ones who had somehow withstood the winds of hurricanes, were just as beautiful as a Montana mountain or a Jamaican sunset. I traveled the path with quick steps, keeping pace with the last song I heard on the radio, rounded the corner quickly, and then saw him – a tall, dark-skinned beauty with short dreadlocks that surrounded his animated eyes and waved gently in the wind like the petals on a stunning sunflower. I smiled as he approached, and he reciprocated the smile.

On the next lap around, I invented questions to ask him, but somehow the act of asking them seemed impossible. It felt easier to meet a man and spark up a spontaneous romance in cities like Paris or New York or San Francisco, places with picturesque backdrops and long lists of well-known books set there. I listened to the leaves crunch beneath my shoes, watched squirrels scurry across the path a few steps before my arrival, and looked up beyond the canopy of leaves at the cumulous coastal clouds traveling across a pale sky. It suddenly struck me that maybe an afternoon in Beaumont was really no different than an afternoon in the so-called romantic cities. Maybe anything could happen anywhere. This thought stuck in my mind and quickened my pace as I shot around corners and pushed through shadows and sunlight, and it was this thought that prompted me to say, "Hello" as the dark beauty crossed my path again.

"Hey," he said and kept walking down the path in the opposite direction.

I watched a squirrel chase his companion up a tree trunk and out onto the edge of one of the highest branches, and I stopped for a moment, turned around, and jogged back toward the handsome stranger. "Hey," I said, sadly a little out of breath.

"Hi again."

"So I had a kind of crazy thought," I said and scurried along beside him. "I'm walking alone. You're walking alone. Would you care to change that?" I looked at his eyes and smiled awkwardly.

I fully expected him to make up an excuse about needing to be somewhere soon, but instead he said, "Sure, sounds like fun."

"Cool. I'm Paige."

"I'm Damien," he said and held out a sweaty hand.

Now what? We walked in silence for a minute while I experienced some momentary buyer's remorse, the kind I had felt after optimistically purchasing a bridesmaid dress in a size eight a few years back. I inhaled deeply, pretended to be absorbed in the simplistic sights of the park, and finally said, "Seriously, you don't have to walk with me. If I'm bugging you, just let me know. I guess I just wanted the company, but now I feel kind of dumb, like I forced you into this when you were enjoying a solitary walk just fine. It's just that I haven't talked to many people this week, outside of work that is, and I—"

"No, this is good," he said. "I'm actually glad you came up to me. I'm not very good at talking to strangers, and, to be honest, when I saw you that first time around, I thought you were kind of cute."

"Oh ... really?"

"Yeah," he said, and I looked up at him and smiled in that sheepish way our faces reserve for first meetings.

"And I thought you were pretty cute too, truth be told."

"Well, I kind of figured that's why you came up to me."

"True, but I could just be desperate to talk to someone, to anyone."

"True, but if that was the case then dog-walking-lady or defeated-by-life-guy over there should have sufficed."

"So you're not defeated by life yet?" I asked.

"Nope, not quite yet."

"And what's your secret?"

"Well ... being twenty-eight helps, and I developed this three day rule a while back."

"A three day rule?"

"Yeah, see the thing is that I work a lot, and my life can get a little tedious sometimes. I started to notice about a year ago that I was falling into a bit of a depression because I never had anything to look forward to. All I did was work and come home and watch TV and wake up and go to work again and so on, so I decided I needed to create things to look forward to, so my thing now is that I can't go more than three days without doing something good or interesting. That way I always have something to look forward to. It keeps me from turning to steel, from becoming a robot man."

"Wow ... every three days? Really? That seems kind of hard to do. I usually live off of looking forward to stuff that's happening months from now. Right now I'm looking forward to going home for Christmas, and that's almost a month away," I said.

"But you're thinking too big," he said. "It doesn't have to be a major thing, like a trip. For example, I'm having burgers with my brother after work on Monday. That's my thing right now."

"Oh, I see. Well, if food counts then I've always got something to look forward to. I eat something indulgent pretty much daily," I said, and accidentally kicked a rock into the side of a squirrel who was standing too close to the path. "Sorry, bud," I said as he dashed up the nearest tree.

"Yep, food counts."

"So this rule of yours kind of reminds me of a game my friend and I invented in college."

"What's that?" he asked and slowed the walking pace a bit.

"I probably shouldn't be telling you about this. One of the ground rules is actually that we don't tell guys about it, but I'm twenty-seven now, and it's all kind of juvenile."

"Okay—"

"Okay, so it's called The Month Game, and we started it during our sophomore year when we were both single and a little bored. The contest was to see which one of us could go the longest, and the goal was to kiss someone every month."

"That seems kind of easy," he said. "But if it were The Week Game, now that would be more of a challenge."

"We added things along the way to make it more interesting."

"Such as?"

"We added an alphabetic component," I said, and he started to laugh. "Seriously, the goal with that was to try to kiss one guy from every letter of the alphabet."

"Do you have a D?" he asked and looked down at me with please-kiss-me eyes.

"David."

"Damn." I laughed and he said, "So who won the game?"

"I did, after about a year and a half. I started dating someone shortly after we came up with the idea, so it wasn't really fair, but even after I won, I kept going with it. I wasn't competing with Abby anymore, but I was competing with myself, and for some reason, I couldn't stand the thought of losing, as though going more than a month without being kissed meant I wasn't desirable anymore. Weird, huh?"

"So the game is still going?" he asked.

"Yeah, and the funny thing is I've actually altered things in my life because of the game."

"What do you mean?"

"I once had a three month relationship with a guy just to keep the game going, and in college, I basically destroyed a male friendship just to not lose," I said. "You must think I'm kind of crazy."

"No, I think you're interesting."

"Isn't that the same thing?"

"It might be, but that's okay ... so ... who did you kiss last month?"

"I've had dates here and there, and I got back together with my college boyfriend after my divorce last year, so that helped."

"And what about this month?"

"The month's not over yet," I said, raising my voice at the end of the sentence to signify defeat.

"You haven't kissed anyone?" he asked. "You do realize it's the thirtieth, right?"

"I know."

"You're kind of cutting it close. You only have about seven hours left of the month," he said. "This must be the closest you've been to losing."

"No, actually it's not. That male friendship I told you about ... well, we went to the fair together. I was twenty-one, and it was the last day of August, and the fair put on this big fireworks show at the end of the day. The finale happened just before midnight, and it was so beautiful. They shot off dozens of fireworks really quickly, filling the sky with colors. I'd been thinking about The Month Game all day, and it was kind of taunting me as we tried all the fried foods and rode rides, but I had decided it was over. After a good, long run, I was going to have to admit defeat. But something about the fireworks changed my mind."

"So you kissed him?" he asked.

"Yeah."

"Did the fireworks make you believe you had feelings for him?"

"Oh, no, that wasn't it. It was more like the fireworks intensified the game itself. You know, like each explosion in the sky stood for the ending of those last few seconds of the month. I couldn't take the idea of losing. I kept looking at my watch as the seconds ticked by, and I felt my heart race as the hand moved into the last minute of the last hour of the month. The problem was that Carlos wanted more than a friendship from me. He'd made that clear several times, and we had just gotten to a point where the awkwardness was gone, and he was finally accepting the idea that we would only ever be friends."

"And you still kissed him?"

"And I still kissed him."

"Wow, that's kind of awful," he said but laughed.

"I know, right? I just couldn't stand the idea of the game ending, so I looked straight at him, clumsily grabbed the back of his head, and kissed him as the last fireworks went off. He thought I was finally falling for him, but really I was just in the middle of a sick competition with my friend, Abby."

"Did you ever tell him the truth?"

"No, that seemed crueler somehow, so I just immediately jumped into another relationship and blamed the kiss on that drunken euphoria that always comes with those last few days of summer."

"You're a little crazy, aren't you?"

"Maybe," I said, and smiled in my playful style of pursing the lips a little on the edges.

"I kind of like that."

"Well, thank you," I said, and he grabbed my hand. I couldn't believe it. An hour before, I had barely been brave enough to leave my apartment, and there I was – holding hands with a handsome man I had just met at the park. I flipped through the mental index of attractive men I had once lusted after and started to wonder what else was possible.

"I have to say, I'm really enjoying our spontaneous date," he said and squeezed my hand.

"Yeah, me too, and it almost seems like the other people here are in on it too, like they're noticing us more than usual. Am I right? Do you see that too?"

He laughed and said, "Well, yeah, but that's because I'm black."

"Ha, somehow I doubt that. Half of Beaumont is black."

"No, I mean because I'm black, and you're white."

"Really? No ... it's 2007," I said.

He laughed and said, "You're not from here, are you?"

"Not originally, but I've been in Texas for a few years." I looked over and noticed a fortyish white woman sitting on a nearby bench staring straight at me with a seemingly judgmental expression on her face.

"Where are you from?"

"Minnesota."

"Well, it's a lot different down here. There's a lot of racial tension in Beaumont, and, to be honest with you, I was pretty surprised when you approached me. People usually kind of keep to themselves."

"You mean to their race?" I asked.

"Yeah."

"That just seems kind of crazy, especially in Beaumont."

"Why especially here?"

"Think about it. Beaumont's about half black and half white, so you'd think we would all be used to each other by now. Besides, who wants to automatically eliminate half the population for dating? Isn't dating frustrating enough as it is?"

"That may be true, but a lot of people here don't think that way. There's still a lot of pain from the past."

"I can understand that," I said. "You know, when I first moved here, I went into a restaurant for a quick dinner and heard a guy working there use the N word. I just thought he was an asshole, and I didn't want to buy food there, so I left."

"A lot of people feel that way."

"Well, I don't, and you obviously don't, so fuck 'em," I said. Damien glanced over at the disapproving woman on the bench, stopped, and turned to look at me. With a face full of mischief and his hand still in mine, he looked into my eyes and swept a wayward wisp of hair off my forehead with his other hand. I wasn't sure if this romantic gesture was for my benefit or just a show for the woman gawking at us.

"You're pretty," he said.

"Thanks. You're one of the most attractive guys I've seen in the park today," I joked.

"That's good news. I hope I'm at least in the top three."

"For sure the top five."

"I can handle that."

By the second half-mile loop of hand-holding, I wanted to let go, but I couldn't stop thinking about the game. I was so close to victory, and it seemed like letting go might diminish my chances of getting a kiss before midnight. Because the convention of marathon hand-holding stopped feeling natural after high school and because, on that day, the combination of exercise and a warm atmosphere caused the sweat from our palms and fingers to pool in the middle of our hands' embrace, I was fully ensconced in hand-holding hell. "Can I ask you something?" I asked him.

"Sure, as long as you're not trying to sell me lotion."

"Oh, God! Are you talking about those soliciting salespeople at the mall? I hate those people."

"Yeah, me too – especially since I used to be one of those people."

"Seriously? Do they make you ask everyone that? Do people

actually fall for it?"

"Oh, yeah. 'Can I ask you something' is a great hook. It sparks a person's curiosity."

"Yeah, until that person has been to the mall more than once," I said. "So what do you actually ask a person if they stop to talk?"

"You never stopped?"

"No, as soon as I saw the bottle of lotion and realized the person wasn't asking me the time, I kept on walking."

"So you're one of the unsellables," he said and shook his head.

"Yeah, I guess I am."

"So what did you want to ask me?"

"Oh, yeah, so what's the best place you've ever been?"

"Oh, I thought you were going to ask me something really serious."

"No, of course not. We just met, you know."

"Oh, I know ... huh, the truth is I haven't really been many places. I was born and raised here in Beaumont and have only been out of Texas a couple of times, and that was just to Louisiana."

"It doesn't really matter. You could spend your whole life here in Beaumont and still not see everything," I said.

"Well, I don't know about that, but seriously, my favorite place is probably Louie's Steak House, and that seems like such a teacher kind of question to ask, like something we would have had to write an essay about."

"That's funny. I am a teacher, and I do make students write essays about stuff like that."

"I don't think I could write a whole essay about Louie's," he said.

"Sure, you could. You could describe the way it smells and the way the low lighting flatters the features of those who dine there on dates. You could easily dedicate a paragraph to the taste of the steak dinner by taking your reader from the creamy, tangy sweetness of the house dressing on the salad to the sea salted skin of the massive baked potato to the tender meat gently glazed with rosemary and garlic."

"Is it weird that this conversation is kind of turning me on?" he asked.

"Strangely, no."

"And, by the way, I couldn't write that essay. English teachers always act like everyone can describe things in such detail, but we can't. My essay would have sentences like, 'Steak is good,' and 'I really like this restaurant.'"

"I know what you mean. I remember my gym teacher in high school acting like running a mile was the same thing as performing basic addition, but it's not the same thing at all."

"Yeah, I noticed you seem a little winded."

"Shut up!"

"Can I ask you a question?" he said.

"Of course."

"Can I have your number? I really enjoyed talking to you, and I could stay here all night, but it's starting to get dark. I'd like to take you out sometime. Maybe we could go to Louie's."

I paused for a moment, not sure what to do, and then said, "I'm here all the time, so I'm sure I'll see you again, and the truth is, I just got out of a serious relationship ... the college boyfriend I told you about. It was a long distance thing, but the emotions were ... anyway, I'm not quite ready to really date yet, so let's just say that if we see each other here again – cool, and if not ... well, I'm sure we will. I just need a few weeks to recover from the last one," I said.

"It's not because I'm black?"

"No, of course not."

"Okay. I actually live in those apartments across the street," he said and pointed to a two-story brick building. "So even when I'm not here, I can see the park from my window. I'll watch for you."

"I'm sure I'll see you soon," I said and let go of his hand. I started walking toward my car, looked back over my shoulder at Damien heading toward his building, and thought about the game. My throat was dry from the hour of walking, and sweat stained the back of my t-shirt and dampened the hair above my forehead. I didn't feel desirable, but the fear of breaking my eight year streak bullied me into shouting out his name. He turned around, and I ran up to him, grabbed both of his hands, stood on my toes, leaned up, and kissed him.

On the drive home, darkness mingled with daylight. The night sky's first star emerged just before the last traces of sunlight faded from view, and for the first time, I started to fall in love with my city. I had my very own proof that spontaneous romantic excursions didn't just happen in places like Paris and New York City; they could also happen right here in Beaumont, Texas.

*

"It's still going," I told Abby, my college friend from back home, on the phone that night.

"What's still going?"

"The Month Game."

"Shut up! How the hell did that happen?"

"I approached this guy in the park today, walked with him for a while, and then kissed him before going home."

"That sounds pretty awkward," she said, and I realized I might be getting too old for our college games.

"Yeah, I guess it kind of was."

*

I avoided the park for months after the day I met Damien and took walks in the residential neighborhoods close to my apartment complex instead. It wasn't that Damien was black, and it wasn't that I wanted time alone. I just needed to imagine a man sitting by his bedroom window, watching the park below, and waiting patiently to see me walk into view.

Chapter Three: Sam

"Speed dating? Really? I can't even believe Beaumont would be doing something like this. Doesn't that seem like more of a Houston thing?" Sam asked.

"Maybe, but it's not like the town is sponsoring it. It's being put on by The Steamboat," I said.

"That upscale bar downtown? I heard drinks there are way overpriced," he said and took a sip of his five dollar coffee.

"We won't be there to drink. We'll be there to speed date. Think about it – twenty dollars to meet twenty singles, but we have to sign up soon if we want to get a spot."

"Can you imagine the kind of people something like this would attract, especially in Beaumont?"

"Yeah, people like us," I said.

There we were – a guy and a girl enjoying a habitual afternoon coffee on a lazy Saturday. Why didn't we just date? The truth is we had, but the experience had been so insignificant that it left practically no impression on us and didn't even register on the awkwardness-scale once we had safely arrived in the friend-zone.

Sam and I met, like so many frequenters of Bayou City Café, right there in the coffee shop. My Minnesota t-shirt caught his eye, and he introduced himself as a former Iowan who found himself in Beaumont for a job managing a new apartment complex that went up after Hurricane Rita. As was his tendency when meeting a woman close to his age and close enough to his physical standards, he asked for my number and called a week later to ask me out.

We got along well enough, but Sam's classic Scandinavian looks were too similar to members of my family and made attraction difficult, and his preference for women with dark hair and mysterious eyes contrasted with my red hair and eyes the color of lake water. We kissed at the end of our second date, more out of an obligatory sense of date etiquette than any real desire, and we immediately confessed to a lack of physical attraction.

Because I saw Sam so often at the *café*, we eventually formed a friendship and even started hanging out beyond the coffee shop. Our two fruitless dates faded into a distant memory and provided us with occasional amusement, and we enjoyed the many benefits of having a close opposite-sex friend to commiserate with.

*

"Ever seen a dog eat a dead animal?" asked Number 3.

"Nope. Can't say I have," I said, searching the room for better prospects.

"Well, it's awesome." Maybe Sam was right. Speed Date Guy Number 1 had somehow worked my breast size into the conversation, and Number 2 appeared to have a drug problem.

"Uh huh," I said unenthusiastically.

"You must be livin' in town. You should see the shit I see livin' out in Devers."

"Uh huh." I looked down at my watch. When the Speed Dating Moderator had first explained the process, five minutes per date seemed like nothing, but after just two minutes with Number 3, I wanted desperately to move on.

In preparation for the night of speed dating, I had spent over an hour straightening my thick hair, applying makeup, and carefully choosing a purple blouse that coordinated well with my pale coloring and the black pants that were just tight enough to hug my curves but still look flattering on my size ten frame. But this guy wore an old camouflage sweatshirt and matching pants. Apparently in his mind, hunting for alligators was the same thing as hunting for women.

When the bell rang, I stood up quickly, forgetting that the women were supposed to stay put while the men moved from table to table. "Whatcha doin', Lady?" he asked. "You stay, and we's the ones that moves."

"Oh, yeah. Right. Well, it was nice meeting you," I said as he left. Before the next guy sat down, I discreetly marked the **not interested** box on the date recorder sheet.

"Oh, my God! Miss Berg?"

I looked up at Number 4, searching his face and my brain to try to figure out why he knew me, but I found nothing. "Yes—"

"It's me, Clark. I was in your comp class last year."

"Oh, right." I still didn't recognize him.

"I've lost some weight since then ... actually a lot of weight."

"Oh. Well, good for you." How was I supposed to handle this situation? I was mortified. I thought about excusing myself to use the restroom and momentarily escape the embarrassment, but it seemed rude. It didn't make sense that a nineteen-year-old had already reached the desperation level required for an evening of speed dating.

"So what's your favorite color, Ms. Berg?"

"Yellow."

"Nice. Mine's blue." I looked over at Sam. He sat just two spots away and appeared to be struggling just as much as I was. His date had a bad habit of frequently fluffing her short, curly hair and periodically rubbing her face while talking to her dates. This nervous tendency of hers distracted me while talking to my own dates, and I noticed that, as the night wore on, the woman's appearance became more and more unkempt.

"Cool," I said and pinched my leg under the table to repress some of my own nervous energy.

"So, Miss Berg, what brings you to this thing?" he asked, and I hoped Date Number 5, an attractive man who appeared to be in his early thirties, didn't hear this guy addressing me by my last name.

The obvious nature of Number 4's question made me wonder what grade the guy had made in my composition class. As a student, I had falsely assumed that teachers remembered things like course grades and specific incidents from students they had taught in semesters past. But, as a teacher, I quickly learned that with over a hundred students each semester, these memories usually disappeared soon after final grades were posted. "Just looking for dates," I said and took a sip of my coke.

"Yeah, me too, but all the girls here are really old. No offense, Miss Berg," he said.

"None taken. I'm not having much luck yet either."

"Yeah, they should really limit these things to people under twenty-five. No offense." I smiled and tried to make eye contact with Sam, but he was fixated on a slim brunette across the room.

"None taken. Hey, I think I'm gonna grab another coke," I said, took a large gulp of my half-full glass, and got up to kill the last three minutes of Date Number 4.

Date Number 5 introduced himself; looked around awkwardly as I rattled off my name, occupation, state of origin, and hobbies; and said, "I'm just gonna be honest, Miss. I'm sure you're a nice girl and all, but you're really not my type. I go for blondes, like her," and he nodded in the direction of an attractive woman three tables down. "Mind if I just sit this one out and take a piss?"

"Sure. That's fine," I said to the only man in the room whom I had been excited to talk to.

As usual, my optimistic approach to life was failing me. I could have been relaxing at home with a movie and a large plate of pasta, but instead I was fielding a series of uncomfortable encounters with strangers and drinking flat coke.

Rather than sit alone and acknowledge the rejection, I too visited the bathroom. I reapplied lip balm, washed my hands for no reason, and stared at myself in the mirror. Why was it that one rejection from a stranger had the power to send me straight back to my middle school self? Before leaving my apartment an hour earlier, I had smiled confidently at my reflection, but there in the bar bathroom, I could no longer see myself, and I wished to emerge from the bathroom with a waifish waist and hair of the silky golden variety that the women in lipstick commercials always had. Luckily Sam was next in line.

"How's this thing going for you?" Sam asked.

"Not good. You?"

"Oh, it's bad."

"Do you want to just leave now? We can pretend like we really hit it off and just bail on this whole thing," I said.

"What happened to your whole 'This will be fun' attitude?"

"Oh, that went out the window about ten minutes ago when my date was a former student who called me old, and then the optimism was obliterated completely when the last guy asked to take a break because I wasn't attractive enough for him." Sam started to laugh. "Hey!"

"Oh, it's not like I'm raking in dates either. The first girl talked about some weird fixation she has with Hitler, and the second woman was my mom's age."

"Nice. I'm banking on that guy," I said and subtly indicated the large bald man with a burly beard who was a little too lively with his hand gestures.

"Yeah, he looks like he'd be a good time."

"Seriously, though, how can it be this bad?"

"Think about it. This is basically the same scene as a middle school dance. You've got the girls and boys separated, and then they slowly start to mingle, but that doesn't make things any better. It just creates the perfect setting for mass rejection," he said.

"Oh, my God! You're right! I remember crying in the bathroom at my eighth grade dance when Joshua said he wouldn't dance with me because he didn't like dancing, and then ten minutes later he was dancing with this other girl. My friend, Shelly, followed me into the bathroom and told me everything changes after middle school, that it gets better, but it's all the same, isn't it? How can it be all the same? We're almost thirty, and we're still at the damn middle school dance."

"You're the one who wanted to come here," he said.

"I know, but I didn't think it would be like this. Did you know it would be like this?"

"Why do you think I didn't want to come? What did you think would happen?" he asked.

"I don't know exactly. I at least expected to have a good time, but just a couple of dates in, it already feels like a disaster. It's like going to a bad buffet. You only need to taste a few things to know that the rest of the spread isn't worth delving into."

"So true ... so true ... so are you sure you don't want to just bail?" he asked.

"Nah, I think I'll stay. I'm usually the one at the bad buffet who keeps trying different dishes even after being disappointed repeatedly," I said and smiled.

"Well, then get ready for some undercooked meat."

Sam was right. Number 7; a curly haired, forty-something, firefighter; waited about two minutes before saying, "Look, I know there's a system in place here. We're supposed to meet all these people; fill out this form thing; check the boxes either 'interested' or 'not interested;' wait until the person in charge of this event gets around to emailing us our matches; then email the ones we like most to try to set up a date; and finally, after dinner and a movie and a drink after the movie, we get to the good part. You know what I mean? I'm just saying, look, I like you, and you seem to be feeling me. Let's just make a plan right now, for tonight, and jump to the good part, you know, seize the moment, make it ours. What do you say?"

"You mean just leave right now and have sex in your car or something? Sure, I'm in."

"Seriously?" he asked.

"No! I'm gonna go get another coke."

During my chat with Number 8, I couldn't concentrate. I was too preoccupied with eavesdropping on what was unfolding between my Number 7 and the woman at the next table. She too expressed her disgust when he offered up his proposal, and I wondered if he was willing to have sex with any woman. She was fairly heavy-set and wore a thick layer of makeup in the gaudy color palette usually reserved for strippers and clowns. Still, he smiled and leaned in playfully when he reached the end of his spiel. As my Number 8 talked about the challenges of his job running a local pawn shop, I wondered how many men were like Number 7, and, for a moment, I wanted to pick up my purse and just head home.

Unfortunately, while giving Abby the day-after recap of my speed dating experience, I suddenly realized that Number 8 was most likely the one real prospect for me at the event, but I failed to notice this because I wasn't paying attention. He was twenty-nine, owned his own business, was attractive enough, and I remembered him saying something about a habit of reading a lot when business was slow at the store. I wanted to go back and check the **interested** box, but it was too late, and Abby advised against my plan to visit every pawn shop within a ten mile radius in an attempt to "run into" him.

Number 9 strolled over in painted-on blue jeans, brown boots, a button-up plaid shirt, white cowboy hat, and a mustache that extended a little beyond the standard mustache region. "How ya doin', lady?"

"Pretty good. You?"

"I'm gonna lay it on the line, lady. I'm here to mend my heart. I done been engaged two times in the past six months, and my heart is pretty doggone closed, slammed shut, you might say."

"Wow ... sounds like a rough six months." I had a hard time getting to a third date, and this guy had somehow convinced two people to marry him within a six month period.

"Oh, doggone, you don't know the half of it." He looked at his watch and started in. "So the first one was Amy. I met her at a church dance-off. Let's just say she liked the way I did the jitter-bug." What decade was this guy living in? "And from there we were pretty much inseparable. She liked my huntin' dog, and I liked her gumbo recipe. After a month, I slapped a little ring on her finger, and we started planning, but then she got all weird on me."

For the first time that evening, I was actually entertained. A close second to the magical feeling of making a connection with a guy was the exhilarating feeling of learning personal information about someone. "What happened?" I asked.

"She wanted to stay over ... at my place. I'm a good Christian, God-fearing man, and I thought I knew her, but she was starting to get real weird. I think she was having impure thoughts about me."

I thought about telling him he might want to rethink those leave-nothing-to-the-imagination tight pants but instead said, "So what did you do?"

"I sat her down and tried to talk to her about it, but she said she wanted to 'know' me better before the wedding. Knowing my heart wasn't enough for that one. She wanted to tarnish our rings before we ever said those vows. Can you believe that?"

"So what happened with the other girl?" I asked.

"That was a more cut 'n dry kinda situation. She turned out to be a fag lover. Took me two months and another doggone ring before that information came out. How in heck could a good country boy like me marry and raise a son with a girl who likes the gays? I tried to take her to church with me, but it was a lost cause."

I felt my face go hot and looked down at my watch to find that we still had a minute left. "I don't think we're going to be a good match," I said.

"And why's that?"

I would later invent wittier lines to say to this guy, but, in that moment, I simply said, "I too like the gays" and ceremoniously checked the **not interested** box on my sheet.

Number 10 sat down, crossed his legs, and proceeded to perform a rather thorough fashion critique of several celebrities as well as a couple of women in the room. His purple, button-up shirt appeared to be starched and made me conscious of my slightly wrinkled collar, and his thick, nicely coifed hair showed no signs of the horrendous humidity happening outside.

"So what do you do?" I asked.

"I'm a wedding coordinator – or, like I like to say – a wedding stylist."

"Interesting. How did you get into that?"

"I always gravitated toward bridal fashion – the flower selection and arrangement, the endless possibilities of venue theme, the dress, the cake, the flow of the event." His pupils visibly dilated as he spoke. "I love it all. As a teenager, I spent hours in bookstores paging through wedding magazines and started daydreaming about being the one to put all the elements together to make the day perfect."

"That is so cool," I said. "Not very many people get to do what they love for a living."

"Yeah, and it almost didn't happen. My grandmother was the only one who encouraged me to follow my dream. She always told me that the woman I marry will be thrilled that I know what I'm doing with the wedding planning and can take care of everything." I wondered how often his grandma's prediction actually held true. Even after being married and enduring a painful divorce, I loved the idea of falling in love again and selecting special details for a wedding ceremony and reception. I remembered a friend complaining when her fiancé had an opinion concerning the color of the tablecloths that conflicted with her own ideas. It annoyed her that he wanted input on the planning process. The women I knew didn't want a fiancé who took over the wedding planning. They wanted to hold the reigns tightly and take the event in any direction they chose. "You see, so many women I work with are with these guys who just don't know anything about what goes into planning a wedding. Some of the guys don't even seem to care at all. Can you believe that?" I could. "You know, a lot of people dream of working in Hollywood, of making movies, but think about it. Movies are great and all, but how many movies do people remember for the rest of their life? How many movies have a long-term effect and warm the heart? Of course making a wedding doesn't have the far-reaching effect on the masses, but it has a much stronger effect on the people who are there to witness a life-long bonding of two people in love." I wondered what effect my wedding had on those who were there. "And then the effect on the two people in love ... it gives me chills," he said and smiled.

"That is very cool," I said.

"Hey, what color is your eye shadow? It's very flattering on someone of your fair complexion."

"Thanks. I actually don't know. I guess white."

"What brand is it?"

"Cover Girl, I think."

"Ah ... must be Pearl Paradise. I recognize it because of the slight sparkle," he said. By this point, I was completely convinced that Number 10 was a classic victim of growing up gay in a region that vilified his sexual orientation. Like several of my students had confessed in writing assignments or after-class chats, his solution was to marry someone he loved but also have to suffer silently over the sexual joys his life was missing. One of my online students wrote an entire essay detailing the struggle of living such a dual-reality. "But I was going to suggest that you might want to consider something with a green or violet undertone. It would enhance your hair color a little and make your eyes stand out more."

"Good suggestion. Thanks," I said just before the moderator's voice cut off our conversation. I really wanted to check the **interested** box for Number 10 and get to know him as a friend and spend time in his world of weddings and fashion, but I didn't want to be the bride standing next to the man who didn't really want to be there.

He shook my hand, said, "I really hope to see you again," and walked to the next table. I paused for a moment and thought about long lunches and Saturday shopping trips to Houston and then picked up the pencil and checked the **not interested** box.

Number 11 had six kids and had been divorced three times, Number 12 played with his cell phone the whole time and only partially paid attention to our dull conversation, and Number 13 had a creepy way of leaning in too closely and whispering words instead of full-voice speaking them. Number 14 talked about his truck too much, Number 15 was obviously a chain smoker, and Number 16 got up to take a call three minutes before the end of our date.

It wasn't looking good. With only four dates left, I was down to the wire but still believed the evening could somehow turn around. Number 17 was neither attractive nor hideous. He, like so many people, lived in that middle-ground world where a high-scoring personality could push him into dateable territory, but a mid to low score would shove him immediately into repulsiveness.

"Son of a biscuit, it's hot in here," he half shouted.

"Yeah, it's a little warm," I said.

"A little warm? If I had tits, I'd be sweating through the front of my shirt too." And suddenly his nose was a little bigger and his eyes a little droopier. I shot Sam a look of sheer desperation.

"Yep, it's hot."

"I'll have to take you up to Dallas for a Rangers game sometime. It's so hot your ass sweat will wash the seat."

"Sounds like fun."

"Well, it is. It's baseball, so it's worth a little sweat equity. Get it?" he shouted and erupted into laughter.

"Yep, baseball's pretty cool," I said unenthusiastically.

"Hot damn, woman! Loosen up a little. We're on a date here." I faked a smile.

"So what do you do?" I asked.

"I bet you can guess."

I really couldn't. This guy seemed to fall under that seldom-spoken-of category of unhirables. "Contractor?"

"Hell to the no! Guess again."

"I really don't know," I said and looked down at my watch.

"Maybe this'll help. Texas declared their independence in 1835."

"Actually, I think it was 1836," I said.

"Lady, you don't even sound like a Texan. Trust me, it's 1835, and I would know – I'm a history teacher. I teach at Lincoln Middle School. I fuckin' love it."

"Cool." I didn't care enough to tell him I was a teacher too, so I just sat there as memories of my own worst teachers flooded my mind, and I felt sorry for the students assigned to Number 17's classroom.

"And, just between you and me, middle school's the way to go. You can still paddle the shit out of the bad ones without it being too awkward. In elementary school, you feel kinda bad about it, and in high school, it feels a little dirty sending the hot seventeen-year-old cheerleader to get spanked by the principal, but middle school – well, that's just right. It's an easy age to discipline." His confidently crisp tone of voice irritated me as he described the creepiest version of "Goldilocks and the Three Bears" I had ever encountered.

"You're talking to the wrong person about this," I said. "My parents didn't like the idea of spanking, so I grew up in a very different environment."

"You never got spanked in school?"

"I grew up in Minnesota. Corporal punishment in schools is illegal up there."

"Damn! It would suck to be a teacher over there," he said.

"I guess so."

Number 18 made bad jokes and laughed at them with a high-pitched cackle reminiscent of my great aunt's, and Number 19 must have bailed early because I noticed the woman at the table behind me sat alone as I spoke to Number 18, and he never materialized during my time slot with him.

I was down to one last date – one final chance to get something more from the evening than a lesson in the slim odds of finding my ideal man.

Number 20 had likely gleaned many checks in the **interested** box as he moved from table to table. He wore a face so perfect in its proportions and coloring that finding a flaw would require one of those magnifying mirrors that women use to get their daily dose of self deprecation. "Hi, I'm Nate," he said with an expression that, for the first time, made me understand what people meant when they said someone had smiling eyes. He was the most attractive man in the room, maybe in the state, but I hadn't noticed him until he walked up to my table. Years of dating-conditioning had taught me to subconsciously filter out men who didn't fall within my field-of-possibility range. I had gotten so skilled in this process that I no longer saw those men who existed beyond my field.

"Hi," I said but felt myself immediately disengaging.

"Do you have a name?" he asked, eyes glittering.

"I'm Ann." *Why did I lie?* I appeared to be participating in the highest level of withdrawal I had ever seen myself attempt. It seemed I was so defeated by the abysmal odds of this guy liking me that I would rather sabotage the thing completely than hope for the kind of man I could never have.

"Interesting. You look too unique to have a name like Ann," he said. "So where are you from?"

"Here. Beaumont." *More lies.*

"Really? You don't seem to have a Texas accent." Either I was a really bad liar or this guy had trust issues.

"Yeah, I took some classes in language homogenization a few years ago at the local career center." *What?* "I guess I'm kind of a quick study."

"I guess so," he said. "Which career center was that? Those lessons might come in handy if I decide to try out for regional commercials. Some of my friends have suggested that."

"I could definitely see that. You have the face for TV. I don't remember the name of the place, but it's the one by the mall."

"Killian?"

"Yeah, that's it, but they may not have those classes anymore," I said. "That was a while ago."

"True, true. Have you ever tried out for local ads? You've got a beautiful face."

I laughed and said, "My hand was in a dog food commercial once. My friend in Austin started this organic dog food brand, and I was the one who scooped out a cup of food for a mini dachshund standing by a crystal serving bowl."

"Sounds like those Fancy Feast commercials for cat food," he said.

"Yeah, she pretty much copied that idea but didn't have to worry about law suits since her commercial only appeared on the product's webpage and was probably only viewed by members of her immediate family." Of course the only moderately clever anecdote I had all night was completely fabricated.

He chuckled and said, "Nice."

"And what about you? What's your story?"

"I'm a carpenter. I do a lot of kitchen remodels mostly." As he talked about his current project, the thrill of tearing something down and rebuilding something more beautiful, I wished I could start our date over again, wished I could swallow up the lies I fed him and just be myself. "I really enjoyed talking to you, Ann," he said as the moderator stood up in preparation to announce the end of the date. "It would be great to get together sometime."

"Yeah, me too. Me too. I'll definitely check the interested box for you, and we can plan something." He smiled, stood up, and initiated a hug.

I sat back down for a moment and pretended to check my phone for messages as he walked away. I stared at the page and considered my options, but they weren't good. If I checked **interested**, he would wonder who this Paige person was when he got his results. He would either not reply or find out I had lied, forcing me to come up with an even more ridiculous story to explain the first lie or come clean and admit my idiotic insecurities.

If I checked **not interested**, I would eliminate any possibility of seeing the one viable option from the evening again.

"Hey," Sam said, startling me away from my dilemma.

"Hey. Any prospects?"

"Nope. You?" he asked.

"Nope. You were right. A total waste of time."

"It's okay. Want to go get a drink somewhere?"

"They have drinks here," I said.

"Have you seen the prices? Plus, do you really want to hang around the scene of the crime with all these casualties lying around?"

"True. Let's go get a coffee."

"Sounds good."

I folded up my sheet and stuffed it in my back pocket, never officially checking a box for Date Number 20. I had entered the evening foolishly expecting a plethora of prospects but left with the same prognosis I had come with. I was still alone.

Sam turned in his results form to the moderator on the way out, but I kept mine and tossed it in a trash can when we got to the *café*. I must have figured that if I didn't turn in the results, it would be like I was never there at all.

Chapter Four: Chris

I should have known when I met him for dinner at five, and he was already drunk. I should have known as soon as I saw him sitting in the lobby in that bright yellow t-shirt with the words **oral skills** in big black letters across the front. I should have introduced myself quickly, made up an excuse to get out of there, and left, but I stayed. Maybe it was curiosity, or maybe I simply couldn't invent a plausible excuse fast enough. I don't remember. What I do remember is telling myself repeatedly that I would never again go out with a guy I met at Walmart.

"Interesting wardrobe choice," I said sarcastically.

He looked at his ripped jeans and said, "Hey, I got these my senior year of high school, wore them on a date, and got lucky. I thought maybe I would test 'em again."

"I was talking about your shirt," I said.

"Yeah, I got this just for tonight. You like?"

"Oh, yeah. I wasn't planning on sleeping with you, but now I might," I said.

He smiled and said, "Awesome."

"You know I'm kidding, right?"

"We'll see how kidding you think you were," he said and leaned over to try to hug me.

I backed away but caught a whiff of his breath before escaping his air space. "Are you drunk?" I asked.

"Not really. I work by here, so I came a little early and had a beer or two to relax."

"You wore that to work?"

"No. I changed in my friend's car."

"Gotcha."

"I set us up over there. Cindy'll take real good care of us," he said and pointed to the bar.

I didn't like the idea of sitting at the bar on a first date, but, since there was no scenario in which I was going to marry the Oral Skills Shirt Guy, it didn't really matter. We took our places at the bar, and Cindy came over. "What's next, Chris?" she asked.

"Get us two shots of whiskey," he said.

"No, I'm not drinking. I have to drive back to Beaumont," I said. He had picked the restaurant, and it was a fifteen mile drive south for me.

"Damn! You're one of them stick up the ass girls," he said.

"Yep, that's me."

Cindy put her hand on his shoulder. "Just one then, hun?"

"Who you kiddin' darlin'?" he said and smiled at her.

"They're on the way," she said and poured two very full shots of whiskey, set them both in front of Chris, and touched his shoulder again. I noticed his eyes follow her backside as she walked to the other side of the bar in short khaki colored shorts that revealed a few stretch marks just below her butt.

"So I don't know anything about you 'cept you buy the strawberry shampoo," he said, still not looking at me.

"What do you want to know?" I asked as Cindy dropped off our menus.

"Where you from?"

"Minnesota."

"Ah, a fellow southern state," he said.

"No. I think you're thinking of Mississippi."

He downed the first shot and said, "Are you sure?"

"Pretty sure."

"Okay, let's get to the real stuff. There are some things you should know about me," he said.

"Like the meaning of those tattoos?" I asked. When we met at Walmart, he was wearing a long sleeved shirt, so the arms filled with dragons, crosses, swords, and naked women were another unfortunate surprise to me.

"Sure, if you like. What you wanna know?"

"Do they have any significance, or did you just like the pictures?" I asked as I opened my menu.

"I always felt like a dragon. Ever since I was a kid and learned about them I wanted to see one. I been to a few zoos, but I guess they don't have them in Texas."

"You know dragons aren't real, right, that they're just mythical figures?" I asked.

"That would explain it then," he said and looked at his arm quizzically.

"What about the women?"

"Oh, I know they're real. These are my ex girlfriends."

"Did you get the tattoos before or after you broke up?"

He paused and said, "I don't remember" and downed the other shot.

Cindy came over and took our order. I chose the club sandwich because I thought it would be prepared and eaten quickly, but he ordered a steak well done and killed my plan.

"But back to what I wanted to talk about ..." he started.

"Okay ..."

"Where do I sign up?"

"Excuse me?"

"To be your boyfriend. Where do I sign up?" he asked, and I rolled my eyes.

"Why don't we get through the first date first?"

"Technically it's our second date," he said.

"Walmart doesn't count."

"I know. I was talking about Applebee's."

"That wasn't me," I said.

"Oh shit," he said and waved Cindy over.

"Yes darlin'?" she said.

"Get me a Lone Star, babe."

"I'll get ya two."

"That's my girl," he said.

"How often do you come here?" I asked.

"This is my place. I bring all my dates here."

"Except apparently the Applebee's girl."

"Jealous?"

"Sorry, no."

"You will be."

"This is your argument for us to date?"

"Is it working?" he asked.

"Of course," I said sarcastically.

But apparently he had failed Sarcasm 101, probably the same year he failed basic U.S. Geography. "Good. A healthy heap of jealousy always works."

"Where are you from originally?" I asked, trying to change the subject.

"Alabama," he said, and I wondered how he didn't know where Mississippi was.

"So how did you end up here?"

"I'm not sure. There's about a year and a half period that's kinda hazy."

"Meaning?"

"We probably shouldn't talk about that."

"Drugs?"

"Somethin' like that," he said and took a gulp of beer. "There's somethin' you should know about me," he said.

"Okay ..."

"I'm a violent sleeper."

"Why?"

"I'm not sure. I been doin' it since I was a kid. I used to sleep with my mom ... nothin' creepy, just kid stuff ... but I gave her a bloody nose one time and a black eye another time, so she kicked me out of bed."

"I meant why should I know that information?" I said.

"In case you want to spend the night tonight. Don't worry, though. I have a futon."

"Good to know."

"Here it comes," he said and pointed to Cindy as she placed our plates in front of us. "Thanks, babe," he said and gave her the commonly used I'm-winking-at-you click-sound with the side of his mouth. "Thanks, babe," he said again as she set down the ketchup bottle.

"Anytime!" she said, winked at him, and flipped her long blonde hair back.

"This looks good," I said.

"And so will you in my bed later."

"Yeah, that's probably not gonna happen."

"Do you know why I asked you out?"

"You think highly of women who use strawberry shampoo?"

"You really thought that was the reason?"

"No," I said and took a bite of my sandwich.

"Oh. Haha. Tricky."

"Why?"

"Why is it tricky?"

"No. Why did you ask me out?"

"You look smart."

"What do you mean?" I asked.

"You're different than girls I usually ask out. Those girls usually turn out to be psycho, so I thought you might be different."

"How am I different?"

"You're not sexy," he said and took another swig of beer.

I paused and said, "Thanks. I appreciate that."

"No problem. I thought you might take that the wrong way."

"Not at all. It might actually be the best compliment I've ever gotten," I said and noticed Cindy lingering within eavesdropping distance of our strange conversation.

"Cool," he said, obviously too drunk and too stupid to detect blatant sarcasm.

"How's your steak?"

"Oh, it's real good," he said.

I turned back to my sandwich. My neck was getting sore from turning to look at him. I had only eaten at the bar once before. It was when I first moved to Beaumont and dined alone at the Waffle House one night. At the time I wished for company and looked enviously at the couples and families sitting in the booths around me, but that night with Chris I noticed an older man dining alone at a nearby table and felt a rush of intense jealousy. I wanted to really enjoy my sandwich, fries, and cherry coke, but Chris's presence was making that impossible.

"I like that you eat," he said.

"Yeah, I like staying alive."

"Huh?"

"You need to eat to survive."

"A lot of girls don't eat," he said.

"I'm pretty sure they eat something."

"No, I'm pretty sure they don't. I dated a girl once who never ate."

"You need to eat. Otherwise you die."

"That might be true for you, but I never saw her eat."

"Trust me. She ate something," I said.

"Just water," he said, and I decided the argument wasn't worth it.

"Okay."

"She was sexy ... nice little ass and a tight stomach," he said. I shoved a few fries in my mouth and nodded. "Not that yours is bad," he said.

"Thanks."

"What do you think of mine?" he asked.

"I didn't really notice." The truth is that when I first met him I had noticed. He looked cute compared to the other people in Walmart, and I liked the way he smiled as he threw a few bottles of cheap shampoo in his cart and approached me. He had bright eyes and an athletic build and hair right in the middle of the transition from blonde to brown that was just a little too long for a guy in his late twenties. I had been having a tired day, and his awkward attempt to talk to me woke me up.

"I'll bet you didn't," he said and pinched my arm.

"Yeah, I really didn't."

He waved Cindy over and held up his empty beer to ask for another one. "Okay, let's get down to the real stuff. What's it going to take to get you into bed tonight?" he asked before grabbing the new beer and taking a swig.

"Yeah ... that's not going to happen."

"But what would it take? There's always some way."

"In this case, there isn't."

"So why are we here?" he asked.

I took another bite of my sandwich. "I don't know."

He stared straight ahead and seemed to be studying his own perplexed facial expression in the mirror behind the bottles of vodka. "I'm gonna need a ride home. My friend drove me to work today and then here."

"I'm sorry. I can't do that."

"Why not, darlin'?" he asked and put his arm around me.

I wriggled out of his arm and said, "I don't know you. I don't ever give rides to people I don't know well."

"You seem to have a lot of 'I don't evers.' Don't ya, sweetie?"

"I guess I do, but that's my rule."

"Then how am I supposed to get home?"

"Call a friend."

"There's a problem with that," he said.

"What's that?"

"I don't know many people around here."

"Call a cab."

"Yeah ... well ... that actually brings me to something else we need to talk about," he said.

"What's that?" I asked nervously.

"I realized after I got here that I accidentally left my wallet in my friend's car."

My heart sunk as my mind did a quick inventory of the drinks he had consumed. "Are you serious?"

"I promise I'll get ya next time."

"You ordered drink after drink and a steak knowing that I would have to pay?" I asked.

"I didn't want to look cheap."

"But – " and I stopped. It suddenly occurred to me that he may have planned it all. Maybe this guy routinely picked up girls at Walmart and tricked them into buying his dinner, and I had foolishly fallen for it all.

"Would you be interested in splitting a dessert?" he asked.

"No, I think I'm full."

"They have really good chocolate cake here," he said, cupping my knee.

I pushed his hand away and said, "I'm ready to take off."

"Damn! The night is young. What's the hurry?"

"I have a lot of papers to grade."

"You're gonna grade on a Saturday?"

"Yep. I pretty much work all the time."

"Wow! We need to loosen ya up a little." Cindy came over with another beer for Chris, and I wondered how much a bottle of Lone Star cost. "This is why she's the best waitress around. See why I wanted to come here?" he said and tipped the beer in salute to Cindy.

"We're ready for our check," I told her.

"Better bring me one more for the road," he said to her and flicked the glass bottle with his nail.

"No, that's okay. We're ready to go," I said.

"Okay, okay. You need to relax," he said to me and mouthed something to Cindy that I couldn't decipher from my vantage point. She poured a few shots for the construction workers who had just arrived at the other end of the bar, returned to us with another beer for Chris, and placed our check in the middle of Chris and me. "Like I said, I'll get ya next time," he said and handed me the ticket. $64! I momentarily considered the consequences of making a run for it and then fished the credit card out of my purse. "I really 'preciate it," he said.

"I bet you do," I said and handed my card to Cindy.

"You sound mad," he said.

"Can we just not talk anymore? I just want to pay the stupid bill and get out of here."

"Okay, okay. Are you sure I can't get a ride with you? I'm pretty strapped."

"That's not gonna happen."

"What am I supposed to do?"

"That's not my problem. You'll figure something out."

"That's easy for you to say," he said.

Cindy returned with my credit card and the copy for me to sign. I looked at the tip line and felt rage burning in my throat as I tried to exhale my frustration. I had never tipped on such a large bill. My whole bill was usually the amount I was going to have to tip on his binge fest. I quickly scribbled in *$10*, signed my name, and placed the receipt face-down on the bar.

"I'm outta here," I said over my shoulder and slid out of the elevated chair.

He left his full beer and followed me. "Come on. We can go to my house and watch a movie or something." I walked faster and fumbled through my full purse, searching for my keys. He was right behind. "At least tell me what I did wrong. Was it the shirt?" I bolted for the double doors and sprinted to my car. "I'm not a bad guy. I swear," he called. I pushed the unlock button, lunged for the door, jumped inside, and pushed the lock button twice.

As I started the car, he tapped on the driver's window and made the roll-down-the-window motion. I shook my head and aggressively waved him away from my car. He retreated, and I pulled the car out and away.

In my rearview mirror I watched him walk aimlessly away from the restaurant and told myself that I would never again go on a date with a guy I met at Walmart.

Chapter Five: Kyle

"Never ask a guy out in Southeast Texas," I heard a woman be-hind me in line at the Dairy Queen say to her friend. "Texas guys like to be the pursuer, not the pursued," she said, and I nodded discretely to myself.

It only took me one time to learn this valuable lesson.

*

It was January of 2008 when I first saw Kyle in Bayou City Café. He was sitting alone at a central table with an assortment of file folders and large black and white photos strewn across the tabletop. His tattered suit jacket and tousled dark hair caught my eye, so I strategically sat at a nearby table in his sightline, hoping he would notice me. He didn't. He diligently studied the photos, took notes in a small journal, and filed the photos into various folders. I wasn't quite close enough to see the pictures, but they appeared to be family portraits of some type.

I sipped my mocha slowly and read the same paragraph in my Texas travel guide over and over before flipping the page to pretend to read another section about the tourist attractions in Amarillo, but he never looked up.

I got up to get an unneeded napkin, hoping he would discover me, see my long red hair and voluptuous body, and be trans-fixed, but when I came back to my table, he was still eyes deep in his work. I sat down defeated and proceeded to pretend to read again.

Why not just talk to him, ask him out, I thought. Guys did it all the time, and I had done it before, but I had been warned that things were different in Southeast Texas. Guys were guys here in the old-fashioned sense. But what could be the harm? Even if he said no, he would be flattered. I could make a complete stranger's day, contribute to the overall well-being of society even. I thought of all the guys who may have been attracted to me over the years but stayed silent from fear of rejection, took a deep breath, and walked over to his table. "Whatcha working on?" I asked.

He looked up, smiled, and said, "Just going through some old pictures, trying to put together a portfolio."

"Ah, so you're a photographer?"

"Almost. I've done a few weddings for friends but no paid jobs yet."

"Gotcha. Well, they look pretty good to me. I think you're going into the right line of work," I said.

"Thanks," he said and turned back to his work.

"I'm—" I started.

He looked up and said, "I'm Kyle," held out his hand, shook mine, and turned back to his work.

"I'm Paige."

"Good to meet you," he said and studied a photograph of a toddler standing by a tree.

I looked over at my table and strongly considered returning to my things, shoving my book in my bag, and escaping to my car, but instead I said, "I'm sorry. This is awkward, but I just have to say this. I think you're really cute. Could we maybe hang out sometime?"

He looked up again, scratched his chin, and said, "I guess we could do that."

"Cool," I said. "When?"

His eyes seemed to search the room for an answer, and then he said, "Let's have coffee next Tuesday at six at Starbucks."

"By next Tuesday do you mean the day after tomorrow or the one a week from that?" I asked.

"Let's make it the second one."

"Okay, let me give you my number ... in case something happens and you need to reschedule." I wrote down my number, gave it to him, gathered my things, and said, "I'll see you next Tuesday, a week after the Tuesday that is two days from now."

He nodded, and I smiled and left with the confidence of a woman who could make things happen. I had walked into the coffee shop with nothing more to do than waste an afternoon planning excursions I would likely never take, and I left with a date planned, and it was all because of my ability to shatter stereotypes and prove that women really could successfully ask guys out, even in Southeast Texas.

*

The anticipated Tuesday had come, and I was lipsticked and dressed in a green blouse that complimented my red hair. Even my toenails were painted in case he noticed them peeping out of my new white sandals.

I arrived at Starbucks a few minutes early, checked my face once more, and went inside. Kyle wasn't there yet, so I grabbed a hot chocolate and a table by the window.

I tried to look relaxed as each car pulled up, and when the car doors opened and the Not-Kyle's stepped out, I fixed my hair, scratched my nose, dug into the mosquito bite on my ankle, and watched the other customers.

The minutes ticked by, and soon it was 6:11, 6:19, 6:23, 6:42, 6:56, and 7:07! I checked my cell phone over and over again. Nothing!

I called Abby. "Hey," she said. "It's over already?"

"It never began. He didn't show up."

"Is there more than one Starbucks in Beaumont?" she asked.

"There's the one in the grocery store, but he couldn't have meant that one. I don't think they even have tables."

"Yeah, he definitely didn't mean that one."

"Oh shit," I said. "There's one in Barnes and Noble. I totally forgot about that. He's probably there waiting for me. He probably thinks I stood him up."

"Go over there right now. Maybe he's still there," she said.

"I'm on my way. Call you later." I sped the half mile to Barnes and Noble, pulled into a spot right up front, and rushed into the store. The Starbucks was packed, every table full, but no sign of Kyle.

I left feeling defeated and got Abby on the phone again. "Hey," she said. "So?"

"Negative. He's not here. I'm heading home."

"Yeah, he probably waited for a while, thought you were a no show, and left. He'll call you, and you can explain what happened."

"I should have gotten his number," I said. "Then I could straighten this out right now."

"He'll call."

"I know. I'm heading home. I'll keep you posted."

"Okay. Bye."

"Bye," I said and placed the phone on my passenger seat. Just as I turned the key in the ignition, the phone rang again. It was an unknown number. "Hello?" I said.

"Hey. It's Kyle."

"Hey, so I think there was a bit of a misunderstanding—"

"Yeah, I just couldn't do it," he said. "I shouldn't have said I could, but you just really took me off guard."

"What do you mean?"

"It's never happened to me before, a girl asking me out, so I didn't know, but it turns out it's pretty far out of my comfort zone. I've heard some guys are into that kind of thing, but I'm pretty traditional."

"You could've called me. I thought I went to the wrong Starbucks."

"I know. I know. I'm sorry, but this is just not something I've had experience with."

"It's pretty normal for girls to ask guys out where I'm from," I said.

"Where is that?"

"Minnesota."

"Well, this is Texas," he said as my peripheral vision caught a billboard for Lone Star Beer – *One more reason to never leave Texas* it said.

"Yeah, I know," I said. "I'm gonna get going."

"Alright. Good night."

"Good night," I said.

I passed the grocery store, did a U-turn, and headed back to purchase my consolation prize: a chocolate cake with thick fudge frosting and a carton of cold milk. I avoided eye contact with the bag boy as he carefully placed my impulsive purchase in a bag and handed it to me. As I walked back to my car I realized that even though a woman could ask out a Southeast Texas guy, it didn't guarantee that he would show up for the date.

Back at home, I shoveled in spoonfuls of fudge cake, raised my glass of milk, and toasted aloud that I would never again ask out a guy in Beaumont, Texas.

Chapter Six: Jonah

Before moving to Beaumont for my job, I spent three years in San Marcos working on a Masters Degree and devoting my free time to my then-husband, Blake. San Marcos, a town in Central Texas half-way between Austin and San Antonio, didn't look like the pictures of Texas depicted in movies and paintings. Instead of cacti and tumbleweeds, residents enjoyed a lush landscape of palm trees, large tropical flowers, and a river filled with white ducks and geese in the winter and tubing tourists every summer. The transition from Minnesota to San Marcos was easy, like taking an extended vacation to a place that was a little too perfect to ever really settle into. Maybe it was because I was so young or because I was so wrapped up in loving Blake, but San Marcos was sealed in my mind as the ideal of what life could be. Like those fleeting moments with Blake where we stared straight into the light of passion, it was impossible to stay in a place that was so beautiful.

The move from San Marcos to Beaumont hit me with a huge thud. Somehow the five hour move that was less than half-way across the state provided more culture shock than the move from Minnesota to San Marcos had three years earlier. San Marcos was a pristine collection of always-blooming foliage and artistic buildings, but Beaumont was the kind of town where it wasn't un-common to see a bathrobed-man outside of his dilapidated house in the middle of the afternoon arguing with a police officer.

My arrival in Beaumont a few months after Hurricane Rita

ripped the town apart seemed a fitting symbol of my own destroyed marriage. Every blown-down street sign and every damaged house served as a strange comfort that first year. It was easier somehow to suffer in a city of so much loss and poverty, and I felt a connection to these people I didn't even know yet. Still, sometimes I wanted to escape, to just stand in the town square of San Marcos and watch happy people dine outside at the local café under a clean red umbrella with the sound of a young guitarist strumming songs softly on the lawn across the street.

*

"I've been thinking," I said to Abby. "Maybe my problem is that I've been limiting my scope too much."

"I don't think that's your problem," she said.

"No, I mean maybe I shouldn't just be thinking about guys in the area."

"I've been telling you to branch out to Houston."

"And maybe I shouldn't just limit myself to guys from my present."

"Oh no, you're not going to get back together with Anton, are you?"

"No. God, no. That's not what I had in mind," I said.

"Okay ..."

"Remember that cute coffee guy I told you about?"

"I need more information than that."

"The guy that I always bought coffee from in grad school."

"In San Marcos? Isn't that like five hours away?" she asked.

"More like four and a half, but you said to branch out."

"Yeah, branch out ... not jump off the tree."

"It's just something I've been thinking about. He was always kind of flirty."

"Wasn't he like fifteen?"

"Eighteen ... which would make him at least twenty now."

"It just seems a little nuts. I mean, how would you even initiate something like this?"

"Well ... I don't know. That's why I called you," I said.

"I don't think I want to be involved in this scheme."

"Come on—"

"Are you drunk? You seem a little drunk."

"You know I don't do that."

"I know, but this is way dumber than most of your ideas. Where did this even come from?"

"I'm just so bored," I said and sighed into the phone.

"So bored? You have your dream job, and you were just dating Eddie a month ago, and we both know that break-up was far from boring."

"I know, but I want to be more impulsive, to really live in the moment," I pleaded.

"Oh, no. The last time you talked about that carpe diem crap I ended up ditching that job interview to stop Sean's wedding."

"That could have been a good idea. We'll never know because you didn't go through with it."

"Oh, shut up! That was a horrible idea. Thank God I realized it an hour into the drive."

"Maybe stopping the wedding wouldn't have been the best, but you never know. Maybe if you would have gotten that job and moved to Warroad, you would have gotten into a car accident a week after moving there and died. Who knows ... my carpe diem crap could have saved your life."

"I doubt that," she said. "It probably would have just kept me from going into insane credit card debt that year I didn't have a real job yet."

"But seriously, don't you think the best moments in life grow out of impulsive decisions – like that time in college when you drove to Rapid City to see that guy you met on the plane ride home from the band trip?"

"Not a good example. My car broke down, and I couldn't tell my parents I was in Rapid City, so I had to put the repair charges on my credit card. I actually just paid that off," she said.

"I know, but didn't you have fun before your car died?"

"Nope. Don't you remember? The guy made me wait at Mc-Donalds for two hours while he ran errands, and then my car died while we were driving from McDonalds to a movie. He didn't want to deal with it, so he made up some excuse about getting called in to work. I ended up staying at a cheap motel by the repair shop, dealt with the problem on my own, and never heard from the guy again."

"Okay, okay, but that was just one isolated incident," I said.

"First of all, we're up to two examples. Second of all, do you want me to bring up the Randy thing?" she asked.

"Not really," I said in a low, defeated tone. I should have let it go but couldn't. I needed to convince Abby, to get her approval of my plan to contact the cute coffee guy, so that she would console me later when I inevitably made a fool of myself.

"Okay then."

"Think of it this way. When's the last time something really crazy happened to one of us?" I asked.

"Probably last month when I won both jury trials," she said.

"No, I mean something really crazy."

"That was really crazy."

"What about something non work related?"

"Haven't you been paying attention? Lately work is my life, and I kind of like it that way."

"Okay, fine. Obviously I don't have your approval, but I still need your help," I said.

She paused for a moment and said, "I was just trying to prevent you from making a fool of yourself. You know this can't end well."

"I know, and I'm accepting that, but I still want to do it."

"And he's way too young for you. Why are you always so attracted to younger guys?"

"If I was a guy that wouldn't even be an issue. If I was a guy you'd—" I started.

"Okay, well it's pretty obvious how to contact the guy – just call the coffee shop."

"Do you think it's possible that he still works there?" I asked.

"I don't know, but that's really the only way to call him. I'm assuming you don't know his last name."

"Actually I do. It's Carlson. I remember that because this guy Carl worked there too, and they used to joke about that all the time."

"And this is someone you want to drive five hours to see?"

"It's four and a half, and Carl's the one who thought it was funny."

"Okay."

"So I just call the coffee shop, ask for him ... and what do I say if he's actually there?"

"That's up to you. I've already helped too much," she said.

*

I stared at the phone for at least a half hour before dialing the number. Abby called twice to see if I had done it yet, and I lied, claiming the line had been busy every time I tried to get through. I played my most manic music and told myself that the true pleasures of life can only materialize if we cross over to the most daring region of ourselves. I thought about the month game, thought about all those times the silly college game had forced me to rip out the colorless pages of a day's expectations and replace them with something better. I wanted to spend a day with Jonah, but it wasn't just for my twenty-eight-year-old self; it was more than that. I wanted to give the future years of myself the gift of remembering a day in San Marcos where I walked beside a beautiful boy who led me back to those most valuable places within me. I didn't want to fall in love with Jonah. I just wanted to remember what it felt like to know I could.

I dialed the numbers quickly, held my breath while the phone rang, and hoped that Jonah wasn't there. "Coffee Grounds," a woman said.

"Hi. Is Jonah, by chance, working?" I said in a throaty voice that didn't want to work.

"Yeah, just a sec," she said.

I felt my hand sweating on the phone and contemplated hanging up, but something kept me there. "Hello?" he said.

"Um, hi. Um, this is kind of weird. Actually, this is really weird, but this is Paige. Okay, you probably don't really remember me, and why would you? You have tons of customers that you see every day. Well ... not tons but enough, and anyway, I guess what I'm trying to say, and not very well, is I used to come in there all the time. It was a couple of years ago. I'm sorry. You know what, if you're really busy, I can let you go. I'm sure you're pretty busy."

"No, we're pretty dead right now."

"Oh, good. Okay, so like I was saying, I used to come in there a lot."

"I remember," he said. "You're the girl with red hair who was always reading something."

"Oh, good. You remember. Yeah, so, like I said, this is kind of weird, but I'm actually going to be in San Marcos this weekend. I don't live there anymore. I got a job in Beaumont, a full-time teaching job."

"Congratulations."

"Thanks, so I'm going to be in town this weekend, and I was wondering if you would want to hang out. I know you don't really know me, so this is probably kind of crazy, so feel free to say no," I said.

"Sure," he said.

"Sure, you're saying no, or sure, you're saying yes?"

"I'm saying yes."

"Oh, cool. Okay, so just to make sure you understand why I'm calling, the thing is ... I always thought you were really cute, and I was hoping we could hang out and maybe make-out or something," I said and furrowed my brow aggressively and dug my nails into the skin on my thighs. Abby was right; I was making a fool of myself.

"I thought you were married," he said.

"Oh, yeah ... not anymore."

"Cool."

"So you're cool with hanging out, even though I'm way older than you and want it to be like a date thing?"

"Sure."

"Okay, cool," I said. "So I'm going to be there on Saturday, should get to town around two."

"Why don't we meet in front of Café on the Square at three?" he said.

"Okay, sounds cool. See you there."

✳

On the last stretch of highway to San Marcos, wide wisps of clouds stood stoically like great shelves in the afternoon sky. I, on the other hand, was not so stoic. Just like Abby had turned her car around before attempting to stop Sean's wedding, my doubts about spending a day with the cute coffee guy I didn't really know were mounting, causing me to consider not showing up. At every intersection with a rural road or county highway, I thought about turning around, but I kept going.

As I drove into town, my stomach churned, and my fingers could barely hold the steering wheel. Making the phone call from two-hundred miles away suddenly seemed easy compared to the task of actually spending time with Jonah. I was always doing this – making quick decisions that trapped me into facing future moments of extreme awkwardness. It had become a habit in college, and I hadn't managed to let it go yet. Still, somewhere within the nervous agony was a fragment of pleasure. I hadn't been back to San Marcos since moving to Beaumont, and when I left San Marcos, I was still with Blake. It felt good to drive through the familiar scenery alone and to roll the window down a bit to let in the fresh breezes of a town that didn't house a refinery.

I tried not to look as I drove past my old apartment, that tiny one-bedroom dwelling where my old life lived. I passed the taco hut where Blake and I picked up dinner after long days of work and school, drove by the proud procession of palm trees that Blake had given names to, and drove on the bridge over the river where we fed white geese on late nights when the hoards of sunbathers had gone home for the evening. For a moment I wanted the old life back, those fleeting years before Blake fell in love with someone else. It was easier in Beaumont to forget about how happy I had been, to immerse myself in a city that held no reminders of Blake. I suddenly realized that it wasn't San Marcos I missed; it was him. And, because I couldn't face the rushing in of old realities on my own, I had called Jonah.

Regardless of our verbal agreement on the phone, I didn't completely expect Jonah to be there, and part of me hoped he wasn't. After all, spending a day alone in San Marcos, home to the state's largest outlet mall and a gorgeous park by the river, wouldn't be so bad. I was prepared to wait alone about fifteen minutes and declare him a no-show, but as I turned the last corner onto LBJ Drive, there he was, standing in front of the restaurant, holding a single pink flower in his hand.

I inhaled deeply, pulled into the nearest parking spot, grabbed my purse, and got out. "Hi," I called out to him as I approached.

"Hi," he said, handed me the wildflower, and wrapped his arms warmly around me. "I was worried you wouldn't show up," he said.

"Really? I'm right on time."

"I know. I was just worried."

"You were worried? That's funny. I was worried you wouldn't show up," I said.

"Why wouldn't I show up?"

"I thought you might think the whole thing was a little weird."

"Are you kidding? I was pretty excited to hear from you. I always kind of had a crush on you, you know?" No, I did not know. Somehow I was always under the impression that crushes on me were highly unlikely. "So what do you want to do? Are you hungry?"

"I could eat."

"Yeah, me too. Café okay?"

"Sure," I said. "Let me just put this flower in my car first." I walked back to my car and carefully laid it on the backseat. By the end of the day, the flower would be dried and preserved as field flowers so quickly are, and five years from that afternoon with Jonah, the flower would still sit on a bookshelf in my office, a sweet reminder of the surprises life can give.

I looked at Jonah and wondered where the day would go. Two years earlier, as my marriage was falling apart in those last few weeks I spent in San Marcos, my trips to the coffee shop became more frequent, and the hours I spent on each visit increased. I often watched Jonah as he moved from table to table with the dishrag, and I wondered what it would be like to kiss him, to brush his long, dark hair away from his face and feel his full lips and tongue all over my mouth. At the time, this idea only existed in the realm of imagination, something that I knew could never actually happen. He was eight years younger than I, and I was married. But, as I walked back to the café toward him, my pulse fluttered in knowing those barriers were falling away.

*

After the lunch hour, the café emptied out, leaving Jonah and me alone in our booth by the big bay window. We hadn't talked much while we had the distraction of the menu and the ordering and the eating of the sandwiches that were prepared and delivered quickly, but after the empty plates were cleared and our glasses refilled, the scene was primed for more meaningful conversation.

"So I know it's none of my business," Jonah said as the waitress wiped down the abandoned table next to ours. "But why aren't you with your husband anymore?"

"No, it's fine. You can ask," I said. "So right before I got my job in Beaumont, I found out he was spending time with another woman. It all started to become obvious when he started going in to work early and staying way later than was normal, and he also seemed really distant and depressed when we were together." I took a sip of my sweet tea and continued, "She was someone he worked with briefly. I found that out later."

"That's horrible."

"Yeah, I really wanted my life to stay normal, to keep the marriage that I wanted to last forever, but I started to feel that pull ... that pull toward truth, so one morning I didn't go home after dropping him off at work ... we didn't have any money, so we shared a car. Instead of going home and getting back in bed for another hour of sleep like I usually did, I pulled the car around to the other side of the restaurant where he worked, parked it in a place where I could see people coming and going, and after a few minutes, I saw him. He came out of the restaurant without his apron on and got into a car that sped off quickly."

"Did you follow him?" he asked.

"No. It was strange. I couldn't get my body to move, like all my muscles just shut down when I saw him leave the restaurant."

"I'm so sorry. That must've been awful."

"Yeah, so I just sat there for almost two hours, frozen in my skin, like if I didn't move I wouldn't have to face what came next, like I could somehow sit still enough to undo what had just happened." He nodded sincerely, and I wondered why I was telling him all of this. I could have easily answered the question in a sentence or two, but it felt easy talking to Jonah. After two years at my Beaumont job, most of my coworkers didn't even know I had been married, and only my closest friends knew the exact details of how it ended.

"So did you see him come back?" he asked.

"Yeah, eventually he did, and the woman actually got out of the car and kissed him goodbye."

"Wow, that's awful. What did you do?"

"I waited for him to go inside, and I drove home. I couldn't bring myself to confront him in front of a restaurant full of people trying to enjoy their breakfast, so I went home and called him at the restaurant. I made up a story about a snake being in the apartment and asked him to get a ride home to help me get rid of it. He came straight home, and I started shouting at him when he walked in the door. We stayed together for four months after that day, but I hated him then, couldn't even look at him or sleep next to him anymore. He moved out shortly after we got to Beaumont, and I filed for divorce after that, and that's the end of that story." I took another sip of tea, sat back a bit, and basked in the excessive eye contact Jonah was giving me. It had been months since I had talked about that morning, and telling it all to Jonah, the source of countless night and day dreams, wasn't painful. In fact, for the first time, I didn't want to erase that memory from my life, and I felt strong for having lived through it.

The waitress seemed to sense the seriousness of our conversation because she didn't return to drop off the ticket until I had concluded the story. "I got this," Jonah said, picking up the bill.

"No, I invited you to hang out today. It's on me," I said.

"Are you kidding? You drove all the way here, and I'm the guy. I want to pay for your lunch."

"Okay, thanks," I said.

*

Jonah stayed in the car while I checked into the hotel I was staying at that night. I wasn't sure if he was signaling to me that nothing sexual was going to happen or if he just didn't see a point in coming in for the five minutes it would take me to obtain the room key and drop off my bag.

Back at the car I asked him, "So how long do I have you for?"

"I'm free all day," he said. "And all night ... not to freak you out," he continued, which answered my question about the hotel.

"Cool, so what do you want to do?"

"It's really nice outside. Why don't we go to the park by the river for a while?"

"That sounds great."

Sewell Park was an ideal place to spend an April afternoon. Everything was fully alive, from the half-grown ducks starting to venture beyond their mother to the deep green aquatic grasses that flourished just below the water's surface and to the softly shifting cloudscapes that sprawled out across a sky-colored canvas. I too felt confident and alive with my long hair waving in the wind and my curvy body dressed in tight, light colored jeans and a playful pink polka-dotted t-shirt.

As we walked down the grass hill toward the water, I knew this was one of those flashes in time I would later wish I had on film. It had seemed awkward to bring a camera, so I left mine at home and instead paid close attention to the way it all looked, hoping I could memorize it in my mind and replay the moment later, or maybe scribble poems about it somewhere in the margins of work notebooks.

"Do you want to sit down or walk?" I asked.

"Let's walk. I had a friend in a wheelchair in high school who always reminded me how lucky I am to just feel the pleasure of walking. Just try it; try really paying attention to how walking feels," he said. "You'll be kind of amazed at what you miss when you're not really there for each step." I watched my feet move and felt the slight sink of my shoes into the soft grass followed by the sturdy strides on hard pavement when we reached the path by the river. He was right. It felt good to be walking.

"It feels weird to be here as a tourist. All those years that I lived here I never really came to the park during the day," I said.

"That's because it's always harder to see a place when you live there. You kind of put off paying attention because there's no immediate need to do so. I try to come here every week, to really be in the middle of the beauty of this place. It was the river that brought me here to San Marcos in the first place."

I pictured him floating down the river on a hand-made raft from some town upstream and said, "I'm assuming you don't mean that literally."

"Actually, I kind of do. Right after high school, I came down here from Waco with some friends to tube the river and decided I wanted to be a part of that experience, to help facilitate it for other people, so I got a job working in the tube rental place and started picking up shifts at the coffee shop for extra cash. I love my job and love hearing the river stories from people when they drop their tubes off at the end of the day, but sometimes it's hard being separated from the source of their pleasure. A lot of times I grab a tube at closing time and ride the river alone after all the people have gone for the day. Then it's just me and the river and the setting sun. You'd be amazed what you see out there when the river becomes wild again – water snakes and large fish leaping out of the water and sometimes a beaver or two swimming around."

"Doesn't that scare you, being out there all alone? What if something happened?" I asked.

He grabbed my hand, looked down at me with his gray-blue eyes, and said, "That's the fun of it. It's the fun of life really, the knowing that anything could happen at any time." It suddenly made sense why Jonah had so quickly agreed to spend a day with someone he didn't know. His spontaneity was far more developed than my own.

"I wish I were more like that, but once something scares me, I'm scared of it forever. I saw a snake bite someone when I was in seventh grade, and I've been terrified of those guys ever since. Our health teacher made us watch a video of a woman giving birth in ninth grade. The point was obviously to scare us out of having children in high school, but here I am, almost thirty, and I'm still terrified of giving birth. The DARE program scared me so much that I've not only never tried marijuana, but I've also never been drunk, and a police officer came to my class in tenth grade to talk about the dangers of speeding. He showed us these pictures of cars wrapped around trees and bloody corpses lying in the middle of the road. To this day, I always drive a couple of miles under the speed limit ... and the AIDS scare of the eighties ... that shit scared me so much I didn't have sex until I was twenty-four."

"Wow," he said and chuckled. "Is that when you got married?"

"Yeah. The thing is, all those scare tactics adults invented to keep me safe as a kid didn't magically stop being scary when I turned eighteen. It's been kind of a problem."

"I just grew up differently. My mom homeschooled me, and she's pretty free in the way she looks at life. We moved around a lot, met people from all over the world, and always followed the music."

"Followed the music?"

"Yeah, she's a musician. Since I came here, she moved from Waco to St. Louis to Miami, back to Waco, and on to Laramie. She's not afraid of anything ... been married four times and still believes in love, lost two children to still births and still wanted to have me, dealt with addiction and poverty and depression, but she always comes out on the other end. It's like riding the river; no matter what happens along the way, I always get to the take-out point. There's always another day waiting for us."

"Until there isn't," I said.

"Well, that's going to happen on its own anyway, so why be so worried about how it happens or when it happens?"

"You make a good point," I said.

"Besides, you obviously know that already. Think about it – your marriage didn't work out, but here you are, walking with me, holding my hand."

"That's because this is easy. It's easy to spend time with you."

He brushed my arm with his spare hand and said, "You're beautiful."

"I'm a lot older than you."

"So what?"

"I just really can't believe this is happening," I said as we came into a clearing with a large swing set and adjoining playground.

"Wanna swing?" he asked.

"Seriously?"

"Yeah, it's fun."

"Sure," I said and chose the swing on the end that was supported by the thickest chains. Jonah kicked off his flip flops and dug his toes into the sand below the swing before pushing off, and I looked behind me to see if passersby were looking at us judgmentally for taking up playground equipment the city provided for its child residents.

"What are you waiting for?" he shouted as he swung down and back and shot upward again.

"I just feel kind of silly, like I'm too old for this."

"Come on! I'm twenty; you're a little more than twenty. It's all the same."

"I'm twenty-eight."

"Exactly! It's all the same. Come on!"

I stood up, stepped back with the seat behind me, and pushed off. I had forgotten the thrill of pumping my legs hard and holding the chains with elbows extended while I glided higher and higher with the wind and sun in my hair. "You're really fun," I shouted at Jonah. "This is really fun."

"You're really fun too," he said, and I watched him as his long legs carried him up and his lean body flew past me. It would be easy to fall in love with Jonah, but I didn't want to. It was obvious, even after just a few hours, to see exactly what would go wrong between us, and for once, I just wanted to keep a connection untarnished and preserve its memory for future hours. I knew I would have no pictures from that day, no photographic proof that the afternoon had existed, but I needed to hold onto it, needed to make amends with my past in San Marcos, to love the town I had once called home for just one more day before leaving again.

*

"So what's your dream life?" Jonah asked me as we walked along the river path, far beyond the playground and further than I had ventured during my three year stay in San Marcos.

I smiled through a sigh and said, "It's been a really long time since someone's asked me that."

"Well, what is it? What does it look like?"

"This is going to sound kind of weird, but every time I've thought about an ideal life, a really happy life, I'm in a house with a room with vaulted ceilings and one of those huge trampolines in the middle of the room. I'm just jumping and jumping, and I feel completely free. It's because I had a trampoline like that as a kid. It was in our backyard, and I seriously spent hours on that thing some days. It's the happiest I've ever been in my life," I said. "I know I should tell you I want to get married again or that I want kids or to take lots of amazing trips, and I do want those things ... don't get me wrong, but I always think about that room with the trampoline when I think about how life could be at its best."

"Then picture yourself in a room with vaulted ceilings," he said. "It will happen."

"What about you? What do you dream about?" I asked.

"Love," he said. "I just want a life filled with love. It doesn't even matter what kind. It could be a child or friendship or a great lover or the earth. I believe the whole reason for our existence is to love and be loved. My mother taught me that. She lives her life for her love of music and her love for me. If I do that, I can't go wrong."

"That's a really good answer," I said and stopped before reaching the ungroomed rocks and uncut grass ahead. "Well, it looks like that's the end of the path. I guess we should head back."

"No, let's keep going. We just need to make our own path," he said, and I wondered if he knew how profound that statement really was. Every great once in a while, we hear something that stays with us and has the power to transform the look of future struggles. To Jonah, it was just an observation, but for me, it would serve as guidance for living. I thought about my life, about all the times when the path I expected to follow suddenly stopped, and I realized that Jonah was right. I just needed to keep going, past the end of what I expected, and make my own path. It had been true when my marriage ended, and, in some ways, I hadn't kept going but instead just stood there at the end of the old path, afraid to keep walking. As Jonah grabbed my hand to help me over the boulder that stood in the way, I knew things were going to be different for me.

*

"Do you wanna just hang out here?" I asked, feeling a little lethargic after a dinner of Mexican food, sitting on the soft bed, back at the hotel with Jonah.

"Are you kidding? It's just about sunset. Let's go watch the conclusion of the day."

"I love the way you say things, like everything is magical or something."

"Everything is magical," he said, grabbed my hand, and pulled me up off the bed and away from the TV I had just turned on.

"Well, I guess this is a good place for a sunset stroll. The hotel has that rural road running behind it."

"I know. It's the best, and the best part is that you can't see that hideous outlet mall from that side of the highway."

I refrained from telling Jonah that visiting the mall had been one of my favorite activities when I lived in San Marcos and just said, "True."

"So let's go," he half-shouted with enthusiasm.

"Okay, just let me get my shoes on."

Out behind the hotel, the huge sky hovered above a seemingly endless field of grasses. The day was going better than expected, but I still hadn't kissed Jonah. I realized he might be waiting for me to make the first move since I was so overbearing while making plans on the phone and because I was older, but that wasn't the way I had imagined it when I thought about him.

"See – isn't this better than TV?" he said.

"Yeah, it's pretty wonderful."

"You should see it over the river sometime. It's like the water and sky become one as the sun slowly departs from view." I smiled and nodded, knowing I never would.

"So how long are you planning to stay here?"

"I'd like to stay all night, if that's okay with you," he said.

I chuckled and said, "I meant in San Marcos."

"Oh, well that all depends. Making choices like that is kind of like writing a song. You don't really think about how long the song will go when you're writing it. You just know when it's over," he said, looked up, and said again, "You just know."

"That actually makes a lot of sense," I said, not sure whether or not it did.

"God, it's so beautiful," he said, extending his arms out and up, making them into tight fists, and relaxing them again at his sides. He almost danced as he moved easily down that country road, and his energy made me more aware of everything – the crescendo and diminuendo of the crickets, the crunch of loose gravel under our feet, the dewy air of dusk, and the way the radiant sky-glow lit up his face. I had brought myself to that moment. I had asked life a question, and the answer was far better than I had expected.

"This is the best day I've had in years," I said, staring hard out onto the horizon.

Jonah stopped walking, turned toward me, and looked down at me with that face I had studied so many times over coffee and a stack of books.

"What?" I said, looking up at him.

He smiled and grabbed me by the waist, picked me up, and swung me around. He set me down and said, slightly out of breath, "This is what life is all about, Paige. We all have to search for moments like this, for sunsets like this, but you already know that. That's why you called me."

"Yeah, and to do this," I said, bit my lip nervously, and stood on my toes to kiss him. Unlike most things in life that I built up in my mind excessively before experiencing them, kissing Jonah was exactly as I imagined it. His lips were smooth, and he subscribed to my preferred method of using the tongue sparingly and only to keep the kiss wet and soft. He ran the palm of his hand from the beginning of my hairline to the back of my head and slowly down my neck, pulling the hair a little before stepping out of the kiss.

As we walked back to the hotel, I wondered if there was some-thing unique about the town itself, if San Marcos was the kind of place you should live when you're young, the kind of place that can keep you safe those last few years before fully stepping into adulthood. I looked at Jonah, watched him grinning at the vast horizon, and realized I didn't need San Marcos anymore. Some-where, in the middle of the intense pain of divorce, I had become stronger. Still, as Jonah put his arm around my waist and play-fully pushed his hip into my side, it felt good to be there for one more night.

※

Back in the hotel room, we didn't turn on the TV. This was why I had made the seemingly insane phone call to Jonah, this night where watching my own life was more interesting than watching the fictional stories on TV. The standard room at the San Marcos Best Western, with its beige walls and framed paint-ings of sailboats resting on a plane of placid water, looked bet-ter than it had when I dropped off my suitcase earlier that day. Jonah's beauty extended beyond his body and made the muted colors on the generic hotel paintings and the paisley pattern on the thin bedspread bloom. I could feel my life opening up again. Jonah's bright eyes and radiantly youthful skin didn't make me self-conscious but surprisingly made me more conscious of my own beauty.

I stood in front of the floor-length mirror and put a little lip gloss on while Jonah hummed a reggae song that was playing on my car radio earlier in the day. I pulled my hair into a pony tail, and Jonah came up behind me. He wrapped his arms around my chest, rested his head on mine, and said, "We look good together." I smiled and nodded, and he said, "But I like your hair better all wild." He pulled the binder out of my hair and playfully tousled my mane. "Are you wearing any makeup besides that stuff you just put on your lips?"

"I put on some this morning."

"You should go wash it off. I want to see you all natural. I bet you look pretty."

"Are you sure? People usually think I look sick when I'm not wearing mascara."

"Is that that paint stuff women cover their eyelashes with?" he asked and lightly ran his finger over my painted eyelash.

Startled, I stepped back and said, "Yeah."

"Go wash it all off. I want to see your face naked." I wondered if he wanted to see anything else naked.

"Okay, but don't tell me I look sick," I said and gave him a playful shove on my way into the bathroom.

I unwrapped the little hotel soap bar, lathered up my skin, soaked a wash cloth with hot water, and rubbed away what remained of that morning's makeup and the residue of the day. It felt good to free my skin of everything it wasn't and stare at my real self in the mirror. In middle school, I had learned how to cover my too-pink facial pigment with foundation, how to stifle my skin's shine by brushing on powder, and how to cover my real eyelashes with dark mascara. Putting on makeup eventually felt as crucial as putting on clothes, and only those closest to me ever saw me without it. As I prepared to open the bathroom door, I realized that, for many women, revealing their naked face was as intimate as revealing their body, and I understood why Jonah asked me to wash all the falsity away.

"So this is me," I said, emerging from the bathroom. "What do you think?"

"Come over here," he said, sitting on the edge of the bed. He held his arms out, pulled me onto his lap, and said, "Wow! You have red eyelashes. You're so pretty all natural."

"Well, now it's your turn. Go wash all your makeup off. There's no way you really look like that," I said.

"I don't think I'm ready for that yet. Let me get a little more comfortable," he said, as he pulled me closer into his embrace, and kissed me. So many times I had wished someone could magically transport me back to the moment before Blake fell in love with someone else and make it never happen. I had spent so many thoughts wishing for my old life back, but as my body pressed against Jonah's that night, I no longer wished for that. I wanted nothing more than to be just who I was, right there on that bed in that hotel room with that sexy twenty-year-old man. "I don't want to have sex tonight," he said and lifted my shirt up over my head. "I just want to touch you all over." I nodded and pulled his t-shirt off, unbuckled my black bra, slid the straps down, and pressed my bare skin against him.

*

I had always known it wasn't San Marcos's fault that things had ended so badly the last time, but when I moved away two years earlier with a marriage breaking and a somber spirit, we hadn't parted on good terms. Driving away that morning, after kissing Jonah goodbye next to his car in the town square, San Marcos looked the way it had my very first day there, sun shining off green stemmed lampposts and streaming over the edges of bright brick storefronts. As I passed the river, I realized that I hadn't left Blake because I stopped loving him. I left him because I hadn't stopped loving myself. I turned the radio up and opened the windows wide as I drove out past the last remnants of San Marcos, and just as the last traces disappeared from view, I sent my whispered thank you out on the wind and back to my old town.

Chapter Seven: Kevin

In the summer of 2008, it seemed like Facebook could do anything. I was a late-comer to the Facebook bandwagon but quickly learned that this website served as a source of free entertainment, a way to connect with old and almost forgotten friends and stay in touch with new acquaintances, a place to share pictures and personal details from my life with many people at once, and a place to learn intimate details about the lives of people I barely knew. What I didn't realize was that Facebook could also take the place of life moments that were previously reserved for private conversations, that Facebook could even serve as a way to break up with someone if a person wanted to avoid the awkwardness of doing it face-to-face or over the phone. I was about to find out that it could.

*

My relationship with Kevin ended over Facebook, but I met him on an old-fashioned set-up. I had never met a guy on a set-up before, but I always liked the idea of meeting this way and often entertained my own visions of introducing two strangers, watching them develop a bond, and eventually toasting the happy couple from my deserved seat at their head table.

For most people, the idea of a set-up is such a statistical nightmare that they dismiss it as a ridiculous waste of time; but after a series of dreadfully disappointing dates, I eagerly accepted the offer when a casual friend suggested introducing me to a great guy she knew.

It was the fourth of July the first time I met Kevin. Daytime temperatures soared to the upper nineties with the kind of humidity that could fog up contact lenses between blinks. I wanted to look fresh and beautiful, but the set-up would take place outside at a neighborhood picnic where Kevin's men's chorus would perform. I feared the familiar images of melted makeup and sweat drenched hair, so I put my long locks in a tight bun and used Chap Stick and excessive powder instead of lipstick and eye liner. I looked at myself in the long mirror glued to my bedroom door and didn't quite feel date-ready but told myself that a set-up isn't quite a date anyway, so I shrugged my shoulders, grabbed my straw summer purse, and headed out.

*

"That's him," Sara said, pointing to the guy on the far left of the eight man singing group.

"Which one?" I asked, feeling confident it couldn't be the guy she was pointing to. A guy that handsome didn't need a set-up. Surely she was talking about the obese guy next to him or the guy in the middle who appeared to be struggling with a mild form of Tourette's as he violently kicked one foot into the other leg every few bars or so.

"The one on the left."

"The one standing next to the guy on the far left?" I asked.

"No, the one on the far left."

I squinted hard to get a better look at him. "Really? What's wrong with him?" I asked.

"What do you mean? He's kind of cute, right?"

"That's exactly my point. What's wrong with him? Why is that guy single?"

"Nothing's wrong with him. Quit being so cynical. I told you. He's pretty awesome," she said.

I stood there studying him, searching for some obvious sign of imperfection, but his appearance was beyond polished. He was tall, slim, slightly tanned, had a pleasant face with full lips and dark eyes, and sported a fresh haircut. His white pants and red and blue tank top looked a little less ridiculous on him than it did on the other guys, and he stood stoically but smiled at the audience during rests and between songs. I stared at Sara for a minute and said, "Seriously, what's wrong with him?"

"I guess he's kind of a dork but in a good way."

"Explain."

"Well, he spends a lot of time doing these singing groups, and I once heard him say that he likes to do math for fun."

"I fail to see a problem with that. Do you know anything about his exes, like why his past relationships didn't work out?" I asked.

"Not really. He had a girlfriend for five years. I think they were pretty serious, but she just ended it out of nowhere. It really tore him up at the time. I think it took him a long time to get over that, but that was about a year ago, and I know he's ready to meet new people now."

For a moment my cynicism subsided, and I clapped along to the group's rendition of "Zip-A-Dee-Doo-Dah" along with the rest of the crowd. Soon they were done with their thirty minute set, and Kevin casually strolled over to us as I felt my stomach somersaulting within me. I was always a little nervous on first dates, but this was different. My perfect day with Jonah notwithstanding, this was the first time in over a year that a guy seemed like a real possibility, that I could feel myself wanting him to like me and wishing I had tried a little harder on my appearance. Despite the hideous explosion of blue stars on his shirt that spelled SING across his chest, my clothes felt inadequate when compared to Kevin's level of attractiveness. I wanted to go back in time and trade my jean shorts and cheap red t-shirt for a more feminine sundress. He seemed so comfortable as he approached us, and his voice stayed steady when he said, "Hey Sara," and "You must be Paige," while holding out his hand to shake mine.

I hoped he didn't notice my unevenly chewed nails or the fact that my fingers were sweaty and swollen from the heat. Meanwhile, his hand was somehow dry and soft, just one more contrast that made me nervous. "It's nice to meet you," I said, and hated the way my voice sounded. Suddenly my mind travelled back to sophomore year of college when I changed my major to Radio/TV Broadcasting at the beginning of fall semester but abruptly changed it back after a professor told me my voice wasn't pleasant enough for radio and that I would have to lose fifteen pounds and dye my hair blonde to have a shot at TV. Kevin could speak slowly, enunciating just the right syllables to bring life into the most mundane statements, but my voice rushed across sentences and only originated in my mouth, unlike voices like Kevin's that started somewhere deep within. "So Sara's told me a lot about you ... well ... not a lot but enough to show me you're someone I want to meet. You did know she wanted us to meet, right?" He smiled and nodded. "Oh, good ... good ... and speaking of good, you guys did a good job singing. You sounded much better than you looked ... not that you looked bad ... I meant your outfits. That's what I was talking about, but you look good in that. You can pull it off somehow, but the other guys ... well, they look a little awkward. Like that guy," I said, nodding in the direction of the obese guy and instantly hoping this wasn't offensive to Kevin. "I guess it's the white pants thing more than the shirt. I mean, white pants are never a good idea, right?"

I looked down at my shorts and felt beads of sweat dribbling down my back under my shirt. "I appreciate your honesty," he said. "I'll tell Chuck that a uniform complaint has been raised. We're getting new uniforms next summer, and he's the chairman of those decisions."

"Well, you can let him know, but I was really talking about the other guys. Like I said, it looks good on you. You somehow pull it off." It was going badly. This was not the vision I had had in mind while driving to the picnic that day, but the fact that Kevin was attractive really threw me off my game. It also didn't help matters that he was so poised because, as a general rule, my level of nervousness had always been in direct proportion to the level of comfort of the other person. If a guy seemed anxious, I instinctively adopted a relaxed personality to calm him down, but if a guy was already calm, I took on the role of the anxious one. With Kevin, this equation did not work in my favor. I was supposed to radiate confidence and class, but instead I was mindlessly muttering like an idiot about his singing group's uniform.

"Well, thanks, Paige. I appreciate that." The sound of my name in his mouth made me involuntarily smile a little excessively.

"So how long have you been doing this singing thing? I guess I don't mean singing. I mean, I'm sure you've been singing since you were born ... well, at least since you were like two. Do kids sing at two? I think I did, but I don't remember. I mean, who remembers being two, right? I guess what I meant to ask ... what I should have asked ... is how long have you been singing in a group ... I mean in this group?"

He smiled and appeared to be taking some enjoyment out of watching me stumble. "I've been in this specific group for almost four years now. I started singing in groups when I was still a kid – maybe around eight. And, yes, I think two-year-olds do sing, and I was probably one of those singing toddlers."

"Hey, I'm gonna go say hi to Candice and Robin," Sara said, and I felt my stomach tighten as she walked away, leaving me to completely fend for myself. "I'll catch up with you guys later."

"Okay. Later, Skater." *Why had I said that?* I averted eye contact with Kevin and dug into a patch of grass with my tennis shoe. There appeared to be absolutely no point in continuing the conversation, but we were both stuck. This was one of the central problems with the set-up idea. Kevin couldn't treat the situation the way he would if I were a more anonymous person and not a friend of his friend. If this had been just a standard meet-and-greet at a party, he could politely excuse himself from our interaction and be done with it, but since he would have to answer to

Sara later, he was forced to stick it out and trudge through the awkwardness for much longer than would be otherwise required. I decided to do the nice thing and give the guy an out. "Well, Kevin, it was really nice meeting you, but this heat is really stifling for a Minnesota girl, so I think I'm going to head out. Good job singing. I really enjoyed it."

"Minnesota, huh? What part?"

"Minneapolis area."

"Nice. I'm sure the summers here are a pretty big adjustment." I nodded and tried to remember which side of the street I had parked my car on. "I hope you feel better once you get out of this heat."

"Thanks. I'm sure I will," I said.

"Well, Paige. I hope I see you soon," he said and stepped in closer to me. I wasn't sure if he was going in for a hug or a handshake, so I just stood there as he initiated the always-hard-to-interpret side-hug. For a moment, I could smell his skin, an enticing mixture of pine and peppermint. It didn't make sense; heat and humidity were supposed to war against the efforts of soap and cologne, but on Kevin's body all the elements appeared to be working together to enhance his scent. I wanted to stay in that casual embrace, to attempt to undo the damage of my clumsy conversational skills, but it was too late.

"I hope so too. Nice meeting you," I said and walked away.

*

An hour later I received this text from Sara: *Kevin said he liked meeting you. He thinks you're pretty cute. Is it okay if I give him your number?* I was completely dumbfounded. I had performed as poorly as possible, but he was interested in contacting me? I would later learn that there are men who prefer awkward women because they enjoy the feeling of having their own confident stature further emphasized, but I didn't know this yet.

*

Kevin was in the navy, something I knew very little about, having grown up in a family that never discussed the possibility of a military career and in a region where many teachers and pastors were suspicious of military pursuits. I believed that being in the navy was simply a career choice, like being an assistant manager of Walgreens or being a college professor. I assumed that Kevin's life outside of work existed in a separate segment like my non-work life did, that when he was away from work he could adopt a more lax persona than the military required, that he could live his own life to his own standards and not worry about what his superiors would think. This may be the case with most military workers, but it wasn't with Kevin.

The first time I walked into his house was after our second date. I was immediately impressed with the amount of cleaning he had done and wasn't aware yet that his house was always kept to such immaculate standards. I slipped off my shoes upon entering, and he nodded his approval. The house smelled of fresh leaves, and all the colors on the walls and furniture and decorations were muted tones. A large model sailboat stood on an antique end table by the big bay window, and the television was hidden in a closed armoire. The couches were reminiscent of the Victorian era with their straight backs and firm cushions and seemed to serve as a statement on the importance of proper posture.

"You must not spend much time in this room," I said.

"Why do you say that?"

"It just looks so formal."

"That's exactly what I like about it. I think one of the problems with modern Americans is that they want everything to be so relaxed, but relaxed people don't get a lot done," he said and straightened one of the family photos displayed on the fireplace mantel.

"But you can't get stuff done all the time, and besides, even if you could, what kind of a life would that be?"

"Well, Paige, I think it depends on where you place your values. I, for instance, have chosen a life of service because I believe in the power of serving a greater good. You see, our lives, when taken alone, are of little significance, but if we all work together for something beyond ourselves, then we can really start to do the work of this nation, of this world. You're thinking of life as being just your little ambitions and pleasures, but imagine what could be done if we all put our efforts together. Imagine what this country would be like." He used his hands a lot when talking and often finished a point by standing with one hand on a hip and the other hand held out, palm open as if in an attempt to disseminate what he had just said.

"I guess I can see your point," I said. "So let's see the rest of this place."

He showed me the guest bathroom, explained that the new cabinet and white tile floor were installed by him, and led me into a small office on the other side of the pristinely white kitchen. "This is where the magic happens," he said, pointing to a music stand and microphone in the corner of the room.

"You practice your singing here?"

"Not practice ... perfect. I never liked the word practice. That word saves room for failure – for error."

"I see."

"The military has taught me that everything has order, that there is a correct way of doing everything. That's what I like about music. It's all ordered with perfect lines of notes and rests and an exact way to begin a song and then end it."

"Huh. That all sounds a little stifling; don't you think? That idea that everything has to be perfect ... doesn't that stress you out?"

"No – the opposite. It's not stifling; it's freeing. When you know how to order your world then you can be so much more productive." What he was saying made sense when applied to the work portion of life. In fact, I had often attempted my own experiments in maximizing productivity by giving myself a starting date and telling myself that, from that point on, I would waste no time and work on tasks diligently until their completion. This line of thinking served me well in school and later during long shifts at undesirable jobs. But the idea of applying such a strict standard to all of life was terrifying, making my mind feel trapped in that little office and my skin overheat under the airy fabric of my summer t-shirt.

I studied his face for signs of imperfection, maybe a patch of hair he missed during his morning shave or redness in the eyes from overuse of contact lenses. I found nothing. "I can kind of understand what you're saying," I said, but it's not what I wanted to say. I wanted to tell him that the best moments of my life had happened outside of the sphere of perfection, those times when I had broken the rules or taken a vacation from schedules or acted on emotions instead of intellect. I wondered if he would ever stand outside of the sphere with me and enjoy the view of life from the fuzzy periphery of a less structured landscape.

"Come on. I'll show you the upstairs," he said.

The nervous energy that had slowly subsided since our first meeting came rushing back, more intensely with each step closer to his bedroom. By the time we reached the top step, I could feel my pulse pounding aggressively in my fingertips and sense the dizzying anticipation of what would soon come. "So this is where you sleep?" I asked, standing in the doorway of a beige colored bedroom.

"No, this would be the guest bedroom."

"Wow! I can't believe you have a real guest bedroom. I mean, who has an actual bedroom for guests at twenty-four? It's great that you do. Don't get me wrong. It just seems like most ... well, make that everyone that I've known in their twenties has guests sleep on the couch or a cheap air mattress or the floor or in a tent in the backyard. Hell, one time I had a friend over at my old apartment, and I pitched a tent right in the living room for her to sleep in. It wasn't even a full-size tent. It was a pup tent. And here you are – twenty-four and with the kind of guest room that could rival a room at the Best Western."

"Well, thanks."

"It's just really impressive ... your house, I mean."

"Thanks, Paige. So why didn't your friend just sleep on the couch?" he asked.

"It was a really small loveseat."

"So why not just sleep on the floor? Why the tent?"

"The apartment had a severe ant infestation problem. The tent kept the ants out."

"I see. Well, that was a clever solution."

Kevin and I had had a lovely dinner at Taco Casa, sat outside on the patio and listened to live music after dinner, and he thought I was pleasant enough to warrant a house tour. I was upstairs, just a few feet from his bedroom, and completely butchering any possibility of romance by bringing up past ant problems. Some people become mute when their nerves take over, but I was not one of those fortunate people. I knew that I was mere inches away from bringing up the always-embarrassing and never-charming first menstrual period story, that I would have to carefully curl my lips under to silence myself and keep that story concealed. I told myself to say nothing, just stand there and smile, to focus on the way his crimson lips contrasted with the beige walls. "So I have a really strange question to ask you," I said. *What was I doing?* I didn't have anything to ask him. I had simply panicked because the extending silence between statements was pressing firmly against me.

"Go ahead," he said.

I searched the room for something to say, found nothing, looked straight at him, and said, "Are your nipples the same color as your lips?" He looked horrified, and I wanted to melt into the bedspread, but instead I went on. "I'm sorry. I wish I could blame alcohol, but you and I both know I only had Sprite at dinner, so unless the waiter has a sadistic sense of humor and a weird habit of slipping strangers alcohol in their drinks, that excuse doesn't hold water ... or, should I say, hold Sprite ... which does look a lot like water ... I mean, if you ignore the bubbles. It's just that I love your lips. Seriously, I can't stop staring at them, at you in general ... and I've noticed, over the years, that lip color tends to match nipple color ... among other things, but let's not get into that now. That would be inappropriate ... not that bringing up your nipples was very appropriate, but it wasn't too bad, right? And I don't want to give you the impression that I've studied so many lip and nipple pairs that I could devise a reliable theory. Of course I've seen enough to devise a theory but not a big enough sample to know for sure that lip color has any real correlation to nipple color. My sample number could have just been a coincidence." I didn't know what to do next, so I kept talking, maybe in hopes that if I talked long enough I could travel far enough away from that first statement and somehow overshadow its significance. "Maybe what I should have asked, if we're staying on the lip subject, is whether or not you frequently use Chap Stick or balm or something. It's just that those lips are so ... supple." Nope. Talking more wasn't doing me any favors.

Kevin wanted order, and there I was spilling my awkwardness all over the place. "I'm glad you like my lips," he said and smiled.

"And your taste in bedspreads is impeccable. Most guys have Chewbacca or tie-dye or one of those blankets made out of blue jean material, but—"

"Paige?"

"Yeah?"

"Want to see where I sleep?"

"Sure. God, I'm hoping you don't have a tie-dye bedspread. That would be just my luck." He didn't. Entering Kevin's room was like entering a mystical oasis of deep harvest hues and antique accents. The large sleigh bed was framed by a navy blue floor rug and a gold and burgundy tapestry tacked to the ceiling that waved gently with any movement in the room. That tapestry invited the room's inhabitants to lie on the bed and look up to study its delicate patterns. All the expected elements of a single guy's room – the sport hero bobble-heads sitting on a shelf, the band posters lining walls and door backs, the dirty clothes strewn across the floor, and the assortment of video games sitting on a cheap bookshelf – were missing. Instead, Kevin's bedroom was actually conducive with a woman's sexual desires and well-developed fantasies, and this made me even more nervous. "So I know you said the magic happens downstairs in your office," I said. "But it seems to me like this is where the real magic happens." I looked at him and sensed confusion on his face, so I went on. "I mean, just look at that bedspread. It looks so plush and inviting ... not that I'm talking about sex ... of course that's not what I meant. It just looks so comfortable. I once dated a guy who used an unzipped sleeping bag for a bedspread ... not that I wouldn't like you if your bedspread were an unzipped sleeping bag. Granted, I didn't like that guy much, but of course there were other reasons for that ... but we don't have to get into all that now. But just look at your room. It's so—"

He stepped in, grabbed my shaky hand, and kissed me. It's highly likely that the kiss came more from a desire to shut me up than a sexual or romantic desire, but it didn't matter. His soft lips brushed against mine like an eraser wiping away all the stupid things I had said, and when he gently pushed me onto the plush comforter and brushed my hair out of my face, even my mind was momentarily released from all its anxious wanderings.

*

My relationship with Kevin accelerated faster than normal, and Facebook certainly aided the pace. After our first date, Kevin posted – *I had a great time tonight, Paige. Looking forward to date two.* – right on my Facebook page for all 130 of my friends and acquaintances to see. After our second date, I came home to – *Paige, you're wonderful.* And after date three, he wrote – *I'm all smiles because of you.* The attention-seeking side of me basked in the public declarations of affection, not knowing there was a flip side to all that public adoration.

"I think I'm going to throw up," Abby told me.

I plugged my cell phone in, knowing the conversation might last longer than the remaining battery life. "It's not that bad. I think it's kind of cute."

"It's disgusting. He barely knows you. I've been to weddings that were less gushy than the crap happening on your Facebook page."

"I'm not trying to start a fight, but do you think you might be a little overly-sensitive because of Judd?"

"No. I told you. It's been almost a year. I'm fine now. I'm just trying to warn you; I would proceed with caution on this one."

"Come on, Abby. He's great. Trust me."

"But what about the whole cleanliness obsession thing and the crazy workaholic thing?"

"It could be a good thing. It's not like the guy is molesting animals. He just likes the house to be really clean and likes to get a lot done every day."

"Okay, just be careful," she said.

"I really wish you lived here. I know you would like him. You should see him – so cute."

"Oh, I've seen him," she said. "All 703 pictures of him."

"You've seen his Facebook? Is his page public?"

"No. He friended me this morning."

"Really? That's weird."

"Yep."

"I wonder why he'd do that," I said and suddenly felt my face get hot.

*

It was just before five, and I was settling in to an evening at home with a stack of ungraded essays when I heard a knock at the door. I answered it, saw a human-sized smiling pineapple standing there, gasped, and tried to close the door, but the large golden body was strategically lodged between me and the door frame. "I'm sorry," I said. "You must have the wrong address."

I heard muffled laughter coming from beneath the costume's cushy exterior and immediately identified the voice as Kevin's.

"What are you doing?" I yelled.

He kept laughing and playfully pressed against me, trying to gain access to my apartment. "I've come to rescue you from a life cut short from ingesting too much junk food," he yelled from beneath the costume and held up a grocery bag. "Did I scare you?"

"You could say that."

"In this costume?"

"I know, but I wasn't expecting you, and dressing up like a happy piece of fruit would be a clever way to drop someone's defenses and kill her brutally."

"I guess it would be easy to conceal a weapon under this thing."

"Exactly."

"So it's not so much about the costume as the circumstances?" he asked.

"Mostly, but there is something a little sinister in the eyes," I said and laughed.

"You're probably referring to his disappointment in knowing that most of Americans live unhealthy lifestyles."

"But wouldn't he want people to eat chips and ice cream and not pineapples ... since he is a pineapple?"

"Don't push the idea too far. So—can I come in?" he asked, and I suddenly realized the embarrassment I would endure when he saw my messy apartment.

"Can I have five minutes first?" I asked, wanting to hide the stack of bridal magazines sitting on my couch, throw the dirty dishes in the sink, somehow hide the mountain of dirty laundry, quickly make the bed, and put away the recently laundered bras that were drying on the shower curtain rod.

"Don't worry, Paige. My place hasn't been spotless every time you've visited," he said, and I wondered if he was referring to the time when a single water glass stood unwashed beside the immaculate kitchen sink.

"Okay ..." I said, and he followed me in, probably thankful that the costume hid his initial reaction to my low domestic standards. "So seriously, though, why do you have that costume, and why are you here? I thought we were doing our own thing tonight. If I'd have known you were coming over, I would have picked up a little bit," I said, standing at the far side of the kitchen in order to block his view of the living room and prevent him from seeing the magazines.

"I have the costume from my three year stint as a Healthy Heroes member."

"A what? What is that?"

"It's a group that travels around teaching kids about the fun benefits of living a healthy lifestyle."

"So what happens if a guy dressed up like a happy ice cream cone shows up at one of the events?"

"I actually did a skit where I beat up a guy in a Twinkie costume."

"Really? It seems like that would just teach kids that pineapples are jerks."

"We did a little back story to prevent that interpretation," he said.

"Well, that was good thinking ahead. So why are you here, Mr. Pineapple, and I hope you didn't drive with that on."

"Of course not. I changed in the car."

"And you're here because?"

"I missed you and thought I'd cook us a salad for dinner."

"Works for me," I said, wondering if I could sneak away to the living room and hide those magazines while he got the dinner ready.

"I won't stay too long. I know you have work to do," he said. "I just figured if I showed up at a quarter to five that you wouldn't be starting dinner yet."

"Oh, not even close. I had a candy bar an hour ago and was just going to heat up a pizza later."

The pineapple shook its body back and forth to indicate disapproval. "Paige, I worry about your choices sometimes." I wanted to be annoyed by his judgmental attitude, but it was hard to muster up negative feelings when the happy pineapple man wearing a crown of green shoots was the one doling out the advice. Maybe this was why the Healthy Heroes program was such a success.

"Just don't look in my cupboard," I said, fearing the pineapple's wrath if he spotted the box of Twinkies.

"Deal."

Kevin finally took off the costume and was left wearing just a pair of yellow tights and a white t-shirt. His already twiggy legs became chopsticks in that outfit, and his face was flushed from the lack of air circulation the costume allowed, but he was still handsome.

"Do you want a glass of water?" I asked, knowing he would probably turn down a Cherry Pepsi or a Grape Kool-Aid.

"Thanks, Paige."

I got out a glass, noticed he was about to leave the kitchen to investigate the rest of my apartment, and blurted out, "So you friended Abby on Facebook?"

"Oh ... yeah. You should be Facebook friends with Cameron, since he's my best friend."

"It's just that she thought it was a little weird, considering the fact that you've never met her."

"Well, you've met Cameron, so you should be his Facebook friend," he said.

"I know. I guess it's just a matter of preference."

"Yeah, I've noticed you seem a little uncomfortable with technology."

"That's probably what it is," I said.

"You see, back in the day, a girl would introduce her boyfriend to her best friend in person, but now the introductions can take place online." I was desperate to hide those magazines after hearing him say the word boyfriend, not wanting to ruin what seemed like the only viable option in Beaumont. "It's so much easier too and more convenient. Just think – I can meet ten people in a minute online," he said, and I suddenly understood how he had over a thousand Facebook friends.

"Okay. It's just that all my Facebook friends are people I know from real life."

"That's your problem, Paige. You see a battle line between face-to-face interactions and the online ones, but both serve the same purpose."

"I can see your point," I said. "Do you need help with anything, for dinner?"

"Just get me a cutting board, knife, and a big bowl and I'm all set," he said.

I handed him the board and knife and pulled out a delicate blue and white floral patterned serving bowl that had been sitting untouched in the back of the cupboard for over a year. Kevin seemed impressed, but I only owned these things because they were wedding gifts, functional reminders of a two year marriage that couldn't even outlast the most fragile dishes.

"When's the last time you had a salad?" he asked.

"It's been a couple of weeks." The truth is I couldn't remember the last time I had eaten a salad. Every time I bought fresh produce, it sat in the fridge for a few weeks, started to become an eye and nose sore, and was eventually thrown away and replaced with a sense of guilt for wasting good food and good money. At some point I stopped trying altogether and just passed by the produce section on the way to the chips/popcorn/soda/pretzels aisle. I was sure Kevin never wasted perfectly good groceries or had to avert eye contact with the cashier as he unloaded gummy bears, chocolate ice cream, Easy Cheese, hot dogs, Oreos, soda, cheese popcorn, and Swiss Cake Rolls onto the conveyor belt. He was one of those my-body-is-a-temple people, but I never understood why aerosol cheese and cookies should be banned from the temple.

"Now, the nice thing about eating lots of fruits and veggies is that it doesn't take long before you actually prefer them to junk food," he said while cutting up tomatoes.

"Are you giving me the Healthy Heroes spiel or just talking?"

"Both. I was actually pretty passionate about that stuff. It made a real impact on how I view making life choices."

"I can imagine."

He stirred up the salad, lightly drizzled the top with low fat dressing, and dished it up on my yellow plates. We ate with the unoccupied pineapple costume looking on proudly, and, even though I didn't particularly enjoy the meal, I knew my mother would be happy to see me doing something so mature.

After dinner, I acted in self defense. Kevin couldn't see those magazines I had purchased at the Walgreens on the side of town none of my friends frequented. He couldn't know that I often paged through them on nights when I needed to visualize myself in white satin, standing next to an ideal man who would usher me safely into a comfortable future. There was simply no acceptable explanation for owning those magazines that wouldn't send a brand new boyfriend running for the parking lot, so I kissed him passionately and said, "We can go to my room if you ignore the dirty clothes and clumps of hair on the carpet. I promise I'll vacuum tomorrow."

*

"So?"

"So what?" I asked, lying next to Kevin on my bed.

"How did you like it?"

"The kissing or the vegetable dinner?"

"The dinner."

"Really?" I propped myself up a bit. "I assumed you were asking about the kissing."

"Well, we've done that before, so I figured there wouldn't be repeated occurrences if there was an issue," he said and smiled.

"Dinner was good."

"I'm glad to hear that, Paige. I know we've only known each other ten days, but I'm already pretty crazy about you."

"You've been keeping track of the days?" I asked, immediately realized I had focused on the wrong part of what he had said, and continued, "I mean, that's how I feel too. Sorry, I wanted to say something about it last night, when we were talking on the phone, but I caught myself. Strange, huh? – That, between us, you were the first to blurt something out. The truth is that I was looking at myself in the mirror the whole time we were talking last night, telling my eyes not to say anything too forward. I do that sometimes, but I'm sure everyone has their own techniques ... don't really know why I just told you mine ... since women are supposed to remain somewhat mysterious, but maybe that idea is outdated anyway. Maybe—"

"Just take a deep breath," he said, obviously sensing my jumpy nerves. "It's funny. I always assumed you were the victim of an on-going sugar rush, but it's been a few hours since that last candy bar, and our dinner didn't have a significant enough trace of sugar to create any side effects, but you still seem a little nervous."

"Yeah, sorry. This is just me. Well, me around you, I mean. I think I'm just kind of in awe of how put-together you are, and it makes me feel like a major fuck-up. Like right now, I keep thinking about the fact that my mascara always smudges below my eyes after making out ... not sure why that always happens, but it does ... so you have to stare lovingly at Raccoon Woman while I get to stare at Mr. I-Just-Walked-off-the-Set-of-a-Commercial-for-Coffee guy, ... you know, the guy who is handsome but in a really wonderfully understated way ... that's your face."

"Paige—"

"Yeah?"

"You don't look like a raccoon. You're beautiful." I smiled. "Now we just need to do something about your cleanliness standards," he said and looked over at the laundry mountain that was so huge it completely concealed the fact that there was a basket underneath it.

"I just get busy. Plus, I have over a hundred pair of underwear, so I can go a long time between laundry days." I didn't tell him that I occasionally wore a swimsuit under my clothes when I ran out of bras or that I had been wearing the same pair of jeans for over a week.

"Don't you think that's a little wasteful? You really don't need to have that many clothes. It's a waste of money," he said.

"But Twinkies are cheaper than pineapples, so I make up the difference." He shook his head. "Well, my bad habits must not bother you too much if you remember how many days you've known me."

"Well, that's kind of an easy one."

"How's that?"

"It's the fourteenth today."

"And?"

"We met on the fourth."

"Wow! Good memory!"

"Paige, you met me on the Fourth of July." Why was I always so stupid around guys I really liked? This had been a crippling factor back in high school, and at twenty-eight, it was happening again.

"Right, right, I think I'm just having a hard time thinking straight after only consuming two-hundred calories for dinner."

"Don't worry. You get used to it," he said. Lying on my side with my head resting against my hand, I pointed my toes and stretched out my body, trying to elongate the places just above my hips where the skin swelled up.

I didn't feel beautiful in Texas. Back in Minnesota the manager at my record store job had once told me, "You're what I would call a northern beauty. Your boobs look great in a tight sweater, but you don't have the kind of beach body that's required to be a sex symbol in a place like California. Yep, you're living in the right climate for what you've got." This idiotic manager's inappropriate assessment of me stuck close to the skin for some reason, and I would often think of the comment when I looked at myself in department store mirrors while trying on new sweaters. In Texas, as summer temperatures grew almost unbearable and locals wore less and less clothing, my body didn't quite measure up. At 5'2" and 148 pounds, my voluptuous body did me favors in bulky sweaters and winter wool pants by retaining its feminine curves in even the heaviest fabrics. But in Texas, beauty standards were different. Shorts were shorter and tank tops more revealing, so women spent hours every week perfecting their tans and keeping their stomachs trim. Texas men weren't looking for a woman to warm the bed at night; they were looking for a woman to admire at the pool.

"We'll see," I said to Kevin and wondered if I could ever live like he did, wondered if I even wanted that kind of life.

"Seriously, Paige, I really like you. I want to ask you something."

"Okay—"

"How would you feel about me changing my Facebook status to 'in a relationship'? I could do it right now," he said, as he brushed a loose wisp of my hair out of my eyes, rolled over, and grabbed his cell phone.

"Go for it!"

"And you'll accept the request?"

"Of course I will," I said, and there we were – a guy, a girl, and a cell phone in the bed. I had no idea that I wasn't only accepting his request to publish our relationship to everyone I knew but was also inadvertently inviting his cell phone into our relationship. After that evening, I rarely had his full attention and usually took a backseat to whatever was happening in his online reality. I suppose he assumed that he had safely secured his status with me, and the initial work was done, leaving him free to pursue his online endeavors.

"I'll wait here for you," he said.

"What?"

"Aren't you going to accept my request?"

"Right now?" I asked.

"Sure. Why not?" My cell phone didn't have internet on it and was basically a smaller version of the house phone many people had already eliminated from their lives. I wasn't completely used to the concept of having a phone with me at all times and often forgot my cell phone on the kitchen table when I left for work in the morning, but Kevin cared for his phone as one would care for a small child, always aware of its location, always showering it with attention. When I first got a cell phone in college, it stayed in the car, only had enough minutes available to be used for real emergencies, and required several complicated steps and a password to even access the dial tone. I had a list of instructions in my glove box but probably wouldn't be able to crack the code even in the face of a real emergency. Freshman year of college was also my first experience with email, and those short-lived and soon archaic early versions of email were awkward and complicated. I remember memorizing command codes and the awkward email addresses my friends were assigned, like *YRBX76B@prodigy.net*. Users of my campus email system had to type carefully because there was no way to go back and change something once it had been typed. You could only erase from where you were and could not return to an earlier part of the document. I blame these older and less user-friendly versions of technology for my fear and resistance to newer technology, but Kevin was four years younger than I, placing him in college during a time when cell phones and the internet were no longer in their infancy.

"Okay," I said, got up, and went into my office to log on to Facebook.

"I can't believe you don't have internet on your phone," he yelled from the other room.

I pulled up my Facebook page, saw that Kevin had requested to be in a relationship with me, clicked the accept box, and braced myself for a long lecture from Abby.

*

The night of Cameron's twenty-eighth birthday, Kevin and I got dressed up to join him at The Wine Warehouse, a somewhat upscale wine bar in downtown Beaumont. We arrived at seven to find an already half-drunk Cameron, a few of Kevin and Cameron's military coworkers, and a couple of girlfriends along for the party. The pantyhose that were a little too small were digging into my waist and constricting my breathing a bit, so I excused myself to the bathroom to pull them up to that place just under my bra.

As I entered the bathroom, a thin blonde woman looked up from the sink and said, "Oh, hi. Paige, right? I'm Robin. I hope this isn't too weird for you. Don't worry – I don't ever even see Kevin anymore. I hope, for your sake, that he's calmed down a little."

"Oh, yeah, he seems pretty calm. Nice to meet you," I said and half-smiled. She dried her hands and left me alone to hoist up my pantyhose.

I found Kevin engrossed in his cell phone, sitting at a corner table. "I met Robin in the bathroom," I said.

"Oh shit!" he said and covered his mouth, either to apologize for swearing or to indicate concern for the situation.

"So how long did you two date?" I asked.

"Three and a half years, and it was more than dating. We were engaged." For the first time since I met Kevin, he seemed flustered. "Fuck! I really don't want to deal with this shit right now. I can't believe Cameron invited her. Why would he invite her?" Kevin's eyes scanned back and forth, back and forth, probably searching for Robin.

"So it was a pretty painful break-up?" I asked.

"What do you think?" he almost shouted. "We were engaged." I really didn't want to be there. Even under the best circumstances, a night with a new boyfriend's friends was an uncomfortable series of small-talk conversations. But this was starting to travel way beyond the city limits of my past visits to Social-Obligation Town. The landscape was starting to get treacherous, and I didn't have a map to guide me back to safety.

"Trust me. I understand painful break-ups. I'm divorced, after all."

"Yeah, well, it's not your ex here tonight. It's mine, and I really don't feel like dealing with this. Did you talk to her?"

"A little."

"Don't believe anything she told you. She's fucking crazy ... broke up with me out of nowhere ... and just because I have post-traumatic stress disorder, and she couldn't just be a good fiancé and help me through it." His previously poised demeanor unraveled right in front of me, and even his face looked less attractive with shadows of anxiety developing around the eyes and a nose that became too big for his face when he wasn't smiling. In my peripheral vision, I saw Robin coming toward us and discretely nodded in her direction to let Kevin know what was happening. "I haven't seen her in two months," he whisper-shouted. "I can't believe he invited her. What the hell was he thinking?"

We just stood there, silently waiting for the awkward conversation to happen to us. "Hey, Kev," she said with her delicate voice.

"Hey, Robin. How's it going?" He didn't look straight at her but kept his eyes at her knees.

"Good. It's good to see you again," she said.

She touched the side of his arm, he looked up at her pleasant face, and he said, "Damn it, Robin! I'm obviously on a date here. This is my – This is Paige. What are you doing here? Did you really think this was a good idea?" She had the kind of eyes that poets luxuriate in, dark and large and eternally expressive, becoming new with each blink. It seemed that once he looked straight at those eyes he lost his composure completely.

"I'm sorry, Kev, but these are my friends too."

"Yeah, because of me."

"We dated a long time. These people are like family to me. You should have expected I would be here. Come on, we went through this the last time," she said.

"Paige, can you give us a minute?" Kevin asked me.

"Sure," I said and scanned the room. I didn't know where to put myself. Cameron, the only other person I knew there, appeared to be waist-deep in his own serious-looking conversation with a cute Asian woman, and I had already gone to the bathroom. There were no good options, so I went outside, headed to the far side of the parking lot, and pretended to be studying the trunk of a palm tree.

When I first moved to Texas at twenty-three, the presence of palm trees growing outside instantly transformed my mind into vacation-mode. The only time I had seen palm trees outside was on family trips, usually taken in the dead of winter and always resulting in a week away from school. That first year in Texas, even the presence of a palm tree in a McDonald's parking lot threw a dash of magical whimsy into an otherwise ordinary day.

Standing outside waiting for Kevin to finish fighting with his ex, I realized that the focal point of the palm tree is the top. My eyes always went there first and traveled slowly down with the cascading leaves, but I had never looked long enough to really examine the trunk, that dull brown asymmetrically notched surface with unsightly hairs growing out of the uneven ledges. I started to wonder if Kevin was like this tropical tree, charming at first gaze but defective upon further inspection.

"Paige, what are you doing?" Kevin yelled from across the lot.

I walked over to him and said, "You asked to speak to her alone. I was just giving you space."

"Okay, well, we figured out a plan. Robin's going to stay here with this crew, and we're meeting Cameron at Chuck's Country Pub in an hour."

"Really?"

"Yeah. You can stay here with Cameron or come kill an hour with me," he said. Why would I want to stay with a bunch of people I didn't know?

"I'll come with you."

*

By the end of the night, Cameron was trashed, Kevin was drunk, and I was still nursing my first glass of rum and coke.

"Hey," Kevin said and grabbed my arm. "Don't let Cameron get these." He handed me a set of keys. "Put them in your purse. Don't let him have them. No matter what happens, don't let him drive home. He'll kill someone."

I didn't want to be in the center of the kind of scene I had watched play out in movies where the drunk guy goes off on the person holding his keys, but I also didn't want another drunk driver on the road. "He doesn't know you took them?" I asked.

"No."

"So he won't know I have them?"

"No."

"So how will I get them back to him?"

"Jesus, Paige! This is not that difficult. Haven't you done this before?" I hadn't. "I'll get them back to him tomorrow. He'll just take a god-damned cab home." He had never spoken to me like this before, but I gave him a free pass because of the ex-girlfriend run-in and the alcohol.

"Okay," I said and put the keys in my purse.

I watched Kevin down two more shots of Goldschläger, sat with him on the outside patio while he scrolled through his Facebook newsfeed, and later pretended to enjoy dancing to the poor song selection Chuck's used every Tuesday for their 80s Dance Party nights.

Right in the middle of "Girls Just Want to Have Fun," Cameron stormed up to me and yelled, "Give me my God damned keys." I was not having fun.

"I'm sorry, but I don't have your keys."

"Bull shit!"

"I don't know what to tell you, but I don't have them."

"That's not what Kevin said. He told me I would have to talk to you if I wanted them back. Now give me the fucking keys. I'm not drunk. I'm fine!"

I looked over at Kevin. "She's not going to give them to you, dude. You'll get 'em back tomorrow," Kevin said.

"Seriously?" I shouted at Kevin. "You got me involved in this and then sold me down the river? Here," I said and tossed the keys to Kevin. "Now it's your problem."

I walked away and watched them fight over the keys from my viewing spot safely across the dance floor. The music was too loud to hear what they were saying, but a lifetime of observational training in deciphering amateur sign-language revealed that Kevin was angry, Cameron was angrier, and the rest of my evening was looking grim.

✻

"Do you have a dust rag?" Kevin asked me.

"What? It's two in the morning. I'll dust tomorrow."

"Ha! Somehow I doubt that. Just get me a rag. Your coffee table is driving me insane."

"How many shots did you have?"

"You think this is because I'm drunk? Ha! It's not because I'm drunk. This has been bugging the shit out of me for days. Why can't you just keep your place clean like a normal person?" he yelled.

"You're just mad because I gave you Cameron's keys, but it wasn't my fault that he got wasted and wanted to drive home. He was screaming at me. You put me in a really awkward situation."

"No! I asked you to do one simple fucking favor, and you couldn't do it. Now get me a God damned dust rag!"

Maybe I should have taken advantage of Kevin's alcohol-induced rage and let him clean my apartment all night, but I was worried he would break something. "Come on," I said. "I'm taking you home."

"No thanks. I'll drive myself," he barked back.

"Really? After you made such a thing of taking Cameron's keys away, you really think you're fit to drive home? I'm taking you."

"I'm not that drunk."

"That better not be true because, if this is how you act sober, we have a major problem."

"Don't talk to me about major problems," he said. "Your place looks like a fucking frat house."

"Then you've obviously never seen a frat house, if you believe that," I shouted back, ignoring the fact that I'd never actually seen a frat house and was gathering my information from what I remembered seeing in movies.

*

The next morning, I found – *Paige, I'm sorry for everything that happened last night. I'll make it up to you.* – written on my Facebook page. I immediately erased the post, not wanting all my Facebook friends to know a conflict existed between my boyfriend and me. Before I left the computer, my cell phone rang. "Hey. What's up?" I said.

"So what happened last night?" Abby asked.

"I was wondering why you called so early. I take it you saw my Facebook page?"

"Yep."

"Damn. That was only on there for less than an hour. I was hoping no one saw it."

"I always check Facebook before work. It's part of my morning routine."

"Damn. I hope that's not a common routine."

"I'm pretty sure it is. You might want to delete that," she said.

"Already done."

"So what happened? And make it a quick story. I have to leave for work in eight minutes and haven't brushed my teeth yet."

"Okay. Here's the quick version. So – we went out for his best friend's birthday last night, he ran into his ex fiancé, got really drunk, and screamed at me for having a messy apartment."

Abby started to laugh. "The friend's fiancé or Kevin's?"

"Kevin's."

"Did we know he had an ex fiancé?"

"No, I didn't know anything about it."

"And he flipped out about your apartment after feeling like crap all night because he ran into her?"

"Pretty much."

Abby started to laugh. "He should see my place."

"I know, right?"

"Hmm ... well, what would you do if you ran into Blake?" she asked.

"I don't know. I try not to think about that."

"I think I'm gonna give him the benefit of the doubt on this one," she said.

"Really? Interesting. That's not what I thought you'd say."

"I really don't think it's that bad. At least now we know the guy's human."

"True. A robot wouldn't flip out like that over a dusty table."

"Yeah, but you've really got to tell this guy to quit posting your personal stuff on Facebook."

"I know. It's happening next time I see him."

*

I wasn't surprised when, later that day, Kevin showed up with roses and an invite to dinner out. It seemed like a bad sign that the first flowers of the relationship were apology roses, but I accepted them graciously, gave Kevin a hug, and put them in a vase. I didn't invite him in, though, fearing he would see my still-messy apartment. After my classes that morning, I had momentarily considered cleaning but couldn't bring myself to do it. Just like childhood when my mother repetitively reminded me to do my homework, Kevin's escalating demands prevented me from appeasing him.

"I'm really sorry, Paige," he said after I put shoes on and followed him out into the hallway.

"I know," I said and walked ahead of him.

"Just slow down for a second. There's something I need to say," he said, so I stopped just before reaching the elevator. "It's just that I kind of lost myself last night. You understand that, right?" I nodded. "I just don't want you to think that's who I am. That wasn't me ... and I don't want you to think I'm not over Robin because I am. It was just so uncomfortable having her there when you were there. I want to start fresh with you and put all that behind me. I think you and I could make this work, and I don't normally drink that much. I just—"

"I understand," I said. "It's okay. Just don't do it again, and you need to know that my apartment is my apartment, and I'm just not going to ever be a keep-my-place-clean-constantly kind of person. I let it go to hell and bring it back to a livable state about once a month. You have your way of doing things, and that's my way."

"Well, we'll discuss that later," he said. "Olive Garden for dinner?"

"Sure."

*

"Let's go for a walk," I said.

"I can't."

"Why? We're just sitting around watching the weather channel. Why not go outside and actually feel some weather. It's beautiful out there tonight."

"It's five minutes to nine," he said.

"So?"

"So I have to be up at 0500."

"So?"

"So lights out is in thirty-five minutes."

"Why do you have to be up so early? I thought you started at seven tomorrow."

"I do."

"So why five?"

"I have to do my morning run, make breakfast, clean up the kitchen, read the morning news, shower, shave, and drive there. It takes the full two hours."

I laughed a little and said, "Can't you just shower after we walk, get out of bed at twenty to six, throw on some clothes, brush your teeth, and head out the door like a normal person?"

"I need to eat."

I opened my purse, took out a granola bar, tossed it to him, and said, "Problem solved."

"That's not a breakfast. Come on, Paige. Can't we just enjoy our evening?"

"That's why I suggested the walk."

"Fine, we'll go around the block a little, but it's muggy as hell out there, and you're not getting into my bed all sweaty."

"I'll just take a shower here before bed," I said.

He looked confused. "And then what will you wear home tomorrow? Your clothes will be all dirty."

"I can just wear the dirty clothes home and shower when I get home. Quit being so rigid, and get your tennis shoes on."

*

After the walk, he showered first and made me promise not to sit down on his furniture in my sweaty clothes, so I stood in the middle of the living room and watched the evening news anchor talk about an accidental shooting that occurred between two teenagers on the south side of town. I wanted to snoop around, to try to find something strange in Kevin's perfect house, but the shower water only ran for a short time, stopped, ran for another short interval, stopped, and ran about thirty seconds more, allowing me no window for safe snooping.

I was spending the night at his place for the first time, but it all felt so calculated and had more of the elements of a school-age sleepover at the strict parent's kid's house than the spontaneity of falling in love. Kevin had asked me to bring an overnight bag, so I packed the purple floral pajamas my grandma had given me, a tooth brush, and contact solution. It seemed awkward to pack sexy sleepwear when he hadn't even seen my breasts yet, but I worried my childish pajamas would disappoint him. I hadn't made it past the third date in over a year, so part of me wanted to escape the sleepover situation with Kevin and return to the comfort of my empty apartment.

"Your turn," he said from the steps. I looked up, and he was wearing the kind of pajamas I had only seen my dad wear, the kind sold in department stores and packaged in clear plastic – white shorts and a matching button-up top with little blue anchors for the pattern. I bit my lower lip to keep from giggling, grabbed my bag, and headed upstairs.

"Just grab a towel out of the closet by the bathroom."

"I can just use yours," I said.

"No, that's okay. I have tons of clean towels. Oh, and grab a bar of soap from the closet by the bath. I have a bunch of little ones."

"Will do," I said. He grabbed a military history book and headed downstairs, probably to give me some privacy. I opened the closet and couldn't believe how organized everything was. It looked more like a display in a fancy store than a closet in an actual home. Two rows of flawlessly folded navy blue towels stood next to a set of bright white sheets. I studied the edges of the sheets, completely mystified as to how he formed the fitted sheet into a perfect rectangle. My linen closet was a disaster. I had long given up on the idea of ordered stacks of nicely folded sheets and instead haphazardly balled them up and set them on the top shelf. It seemed pointless to devote a lot of time to the appearance of a closed closet, and why fold something that's usually hidden under a blanket?

I grabbed a towel, headed into the bathroom, opened the closet by the bath, and there it was – a black handgun sitting right next to the little bars of soap. "Holy shit," I said under my breath.

Throughout my shower, I kept thinking about the fact that the gun was there. I had never seen a gun up close before. Outside of museum displays, guns, to me, were always more of a concept than a reality, something people kept hidden in their homes but something that was never seen. I knew Kevin carried a gun for his job but couldn't understand what one was doing in the bathroom closet. I needed to know, so I skipped conditioning my hair, soaped up and rinsed off quickly, toweled off, dressed, and headed downstairs to ask him. "Hey, honey. All clean?" he said when he saw me.

"Yeah, so I noticed something in your closet," I said and scratched my wet head. "Why do you have a gun in there?"

"Oh, that? Paige, you don't have to be afraid of guns. They're not dangerous." *Not dangerous?* Wasn't danger the point of weapons?

"But why do you have it in the bathroom closet?"

"I have them all over. They're to protect us," he said. "Come on, I'll show you." The guy-who-has-an-absurd-number-of-guns-in-his-home tour began in the bedroom where he lifted up the mattress to reveal the first one, slid a stack of books off the shelf to show the second, rummaged around in the underwear drawer to unveil the third, and pulled the fourth out of a pocket in a decorative pillow sitting on the window ledge. We then headed downstairs to see gun number five behind the kitchen utensil caddy, gun six in the bottom of an artificial potted plant, gun seven behind the toilet in the guest bathroom, and gun eight on the top shelf of the office closet.

"Why do you have all these?"

"For protection."

"Are they loaded?"

"Of course," he said. "How would they protect us if they weren't loaded?" I again felt nervous, but this time it had nothing to do with his good looks and everything to do with the arsenal surrounding me. I had heard the stereotypes, the claims that Texas men loved guns and had bigger collections than men in the other states, but I had dismissed these claims and assumed they were a classic case of exaggeration. But there I was, standing in the middle of the stereotype, staring right at the proof that everything really was bigger in Texas, including gun collections.

"Yeah, good point," I said.

"Just don't think about it. It's getting late. Let's go to bed," he said and took my hand.

Up in his room, the desktop fan filled the air with soft breeze and made the tapestry above the bed ripple like a large sail at sea. The lights were turned out, but the glow of a street lamp outside the window bled through the curtain and dimly lit the room. I looked over at his dark eyes and listened to the song of the fabric fluttering in the wind, and we weren't in his room anymore. We were a hundred miles away, floating somewhere in the Gulf of Mexico. His bed became the boat, and the blue carpet became the dark night waters that held us. I imagined pirates on nearby ships, pictured them trying to throw us overboard, and suddenly the presence of weapons didn't scare but soothed me. Kevin's masculinity, his military expertise, and his authoritative personality somehow made me feel safe, made me more aware of my femininity and my vulnerability.

Outside it started to rain, but we were dry beneath the sail. Outside the street light flickered, and the shifting shadows on the walls were the sky in those last fleeting moments of light just between dusk and darkness. As Kevin kissed me deeply and pulled my pajama shirt over my head, I knew we were drifting dangerously close to falling in love.

*

"So last night must have turned out pretty good," Abby said.

"Yeah, it was pretty great ... other than having to get up at 5:30."

"You got up at 5:30? What have you been doing the last five hours?"

"I said I got up at 5:30, but I didn't stay up. I got up when he did, drove home half asleep, put my pajamas back on, went back to bed, and just woke up now."

"Oh, okay. Well, sorry I woke you."

"It's okay. I need to get stuff done before my classes anyway. My place is kind of a disaster."

"Yes, I've heard," she said and laughed. "Well, I'm glad that you're happy, but don't you think saying 'I love you' is a little insane, considering it's only been three weeks?"

"Saying 'I love you?' What are you talking about? We didn't say 'I love you.' We went for a walk, showered, fooled around a little, and went to sleep. Well ... he went to sleep. I stared at the ceiling for three hours. Seriously, when I get more comfortable around him, I'm definitely sneaking downstairs to watch TV when he turns the lights out. I mean, who can fall asleep before eleven?"

"He didn't tell you he loves you last night?" she asked.

"No. Why?"

"I'm assuming you haven't checked your Facebook yet?" she said and started laughing.

"Oh crap. What did he do?"

"You want me to read it to you?"

"Yes!" Any morning grogginess I had was gone. I was sitting straight up with my back against the wall, my shaking hand clutching the cold phone, and my feet dancing nervously under the sheet.

"Okay, I got it. He says, *'Paige, last night was one of the best nights of my life. I can't believe I'm already falling in love with you.'*"

"He wrote that on my Facebook page? You mean that it's public for everyone to see?"

"Yeah. What else would it be? I didn't hack into your email, if that's what you mean."

"I know. This is just seriously insane. I can't believe my boyfriend tells me he's in love with me, and you're the first to know?"

"Oh, I highly doubt that. He posted this at six a.m., and I didn't see it until about ten minutes ago. I'm probably more like the fortieth person to know," she said and started to laugh again.

"Shut up!"

"I'm sorry, but this is really funny."

"Maybe I'm looking at it all wrong. Think about it, the guy said he loves me. Does it really matter whether it happened in person or over Facebook?"

"The correct answer would be yes. It does matter. Look, this is going to sound bad, but it kind of seems like he's in a relationship with you more to be seen in a relationship than to actually be in the relationship."

"Huh?"

"Okay, look at it this way – is it possible that he wants people to know, for some reason, that he has a girlfriend, that he's all happy and falling in love and stuff?"

Just then Robin's eyes came to mind. I sprung out of bed and bounded into my office to turn on the computer. "You may be right. Otherwise why would he tell me these serious things over a public forum?" The computer loaded up, and I clicked the internet icon. "If he's friends with his ex on Facebook, we might have a serious problem."

"What's her name? I'll look."

"Already on it. Just give me a second," I said, signed into Facebook, clicked on Kevin's page, and searched his friend list for Robin. "Nope. Nothing."

"Weird. Then it really doesn't make sense. Could he just be so clueless that he doesn't understand basic principles of human interaction?" she asked.

"I guess so," I said and sighed my relief audibly into the phone.

*

After I hung up, I sat and stared at the screen, trying to decide what to do. Instinct and fear of embarrassment told me to delete the *I love you*, but that option seemed risky. I clicked on Kevin's photo, looked at his brown eyes, and told myself that the emotion was the same whether it was expressed through pressing computer keys or through a prolonged gaze followed by a half whispered "I'm falling in love with you, Paige," but it wasn't the same.

I had noticed a shift in human behavior in the months leading up to my relationship with Kevin. It seemed that people couldn't sit still anymore, couldn't focus on one thing, and I blamed technology. Its ability to deliver instant gratification in steady bursts throughout the day was starting to hinder our need for tranquil moments of solitude and our need for connections with others through one-on-one conversations. Instead, the cell phone was always present, always partially stealing the attention of its owner. Instead of meeting a friend for a long walk with meaningful conversation, people settled for a series of short text messages coming from several friends at once. Instead of letting a long friendship slowly slip into the realm of romance, people scrolled through pictures of strangers to search for "the one." Even the pleasure of shopping, of feeling fabrics first-hand and knowing the way the clothing clings to our skin, was being replaced with online shopping.

Kevin was comfortable in this technology-driven world, but I wasn't. I wanted to stand in the moment, to experience life head-on, but he was always poised to leap into the next hour. Everything was moving too fast for me, and I didn't want to chat with six people at once over a Facebook account. I longed to sit with a coffee across from Kevin, to watch the way his eyes flickered when he talked about the places he'd been, but his eyes were always down, scrolling through the images on his cell phone.

I wanted to tell him that the best moments in life are not associated with texts or Facebook or online shopping. These things are not cinematic enough to endure the future weeding out of memories. What will remain are those late night conversations in cars that last until dawn and end in kisses, trips to places that change the way we see the world, and sunsets seen in solitude when we realize the beauty of an ocean horizon.

That summer, as I watched humanity shift to become more and more focused on technology, I felt like I was watching the lake of human intimacy dry up. My college students pulled out their phone immediately after class or got lost in the music on their iPod while walking across campus. I wanted to watch them explore each other instead, to view the rare pleasure of a pair of lovers laughing about a private joke or to see a group of classmates discussing an assignment. I wanted them to notice the lush landscape of tropical trees on campus, but they couldn't because they were too busy staring at their phones.

I stared at the *I love you*, the black emotionless letters on the screen, and knew that the initial inner-rush typically felt from such a declaration would never happen in our relationship.

*

By the time I saw Kevin that evening, I had chewed most of my nails down to the nub, cut myself three times while shaving my legs, unintentionally plucked too many hairs out of my left eyebrow, and spilled grape Kool-Aid all over the stack of essays I was working through. I was a mess. I wasn't sure if what I felt was romantic excitement or repulsion, didn't know how to act when I saw him, and questioned the sanity of a person who would tell a girl he loved her for the first time over the internet.

"Hey," he said after I opened the door.

"Hey."

"So I'm assuming you already ate since it's after seven. Sorry, I was held up at rehearsal."

"No, it's fine. What do you want to do?" I asked.

"Let's watch one of those war documentaries I told you about."

I considered confessing my intense fear of viewing violence but instead said, "I think we can do better than that. Let's do something more spontaneous."

"Well, it's almost bed time. That's why I suggested a movie. What did you have in mind?"

Not sure what to say, I blurted out, "Let's go to the beach."

"The beach? What beach? Galveston is an hour and a half away, and it's almost sunset."

"It's only seven. Sunset isn't until about nine, and I wasn't thinking about Galveston. Let's go to Louisiana. It's a little closer."

"Come on, Paige. Louisiana is a dump, and it's too late to be driving out of town. I have to work tomorrow."

Even though I was four years older than Kevin, I felt like a child begging for permission. As I stood shoeless in the open doorway, he towered over me with a look of disapproval on his face, so I grabbed my highest heels off the shoe rack by the door, stepped into them, looked him in the eyes, and said, "Louisiana is beautiful, and you could lighten up a bit. Where's your spontaneity? Where's your fun-loving side?"

"Spontaneity is looked down upon in the military. Productive people always have a plan."

"But I don't want to be productive tonight. I want to have a night adventure, see something unexpected, hear the waves pounding against the sand in the wind. Come on," I pleaded.

He looked uncomfortable and annoyed but said," Fine, but you're driving."

*

Our relationship seemed to progress quicker online than in face-to-face life. I didn't know if I should bring up the Facebook post and wondered if his agitation was due to our unplanned beach journey or my silence concerning the *I love you*. Rather than say something real, I said, "You know those news stories that say someone got in a car accident because they lost control of the car?"

"Yeah," he said.

"I always wondered about that. I mean, how does a person lose control of a car? Don't you think it's actually suicide? I've been driving a long time and have always had control of my car."

"I don't know. Do we have to talk about this?"

"Sorry, it's just something I think about. I guess it's like wondering what it would feel like to drive off a high bridge, what those last seconds before impact would feel like. Do you die on impact or by drowning?" I asked as we approached the big bridge that would take us to the gulf and the Louisiana border.

"Jesus, Paige! Are you trying to scare me? Can we please talk about something else or put the radio on?"

"Sorry, I wasn't saying I wanted to drive off the bridge," I said as we reached the top and caught the first view of open water. "It's just a thought I had." I rolled the window down and said, "Don't you love the smell of the ocean?"

"That's not the ocean. It's Sabine Pass, and it smells like Louisiana."

"Well, we're not there quite yet. Have you ever been to the Louisiana coast? It's really beautiful and in a different way than Galveston. Sure, Galveston has nice hotels and seafood restaurants with outdoor ocean-view seating and gift shops, but the Louisiana coast has none of that."

"You're not really selling it for me," he said.

"I guess it's the difference between a place that is completely altered by man and a place that is left alone. Other than the Arctic Ocean coast, Louisiana might be the most natural beach. No one goes there, so it stays wild."

"You're acting like development, like man's improvements are a bad thing, but that's what makes the world ordered and comfortable."

"And I'm all about that most of the time, but sometimes it feels so good to escape all that and stand somewhere free of man's influence. One time I saw a dead dolphin washed up on shore with its side chewed out by scavengers. In Galveston, things like that are immediately removed and never seen by tourists."

"And this is your argument for the Louisiana beach, the possibility of seeing a dead dolphin?"

"That was just an example. I was only trying to illustrate the fact that this place is real, like being there four-hundred years ago. You'll see," I said and turned on the radio.

*

As we pulled up to the beach, the sunset was in full bloom. I hid my purse under the seat, kicked off my heels, and raced down to the sand. As predicted, we were the only ones there. With the nearest town miles away, the Louisiana coast provided the necessary seclusion to spark romantic magic. A beach softly lit by the sun's last splashes was a far superior scene for I love yous than a viewing of a war documentary.

"This is disgusting. There's seaweed everywhere," he said.

"This is a natural beach. Seaweed is inevitable. Just look beyond that. Look at the sky and the waves. Look at me," I said, trying to set the scene.

"A natural beach, huh? How natural is this?" he said and picked up a rusted beer can. I wanted to slap him, but, more than that, I wanted to kiss him. He looked so handsome in his khaki shorts and red polo, with his tanned skin and angular face, and somehow this overshadowed what he said. Maybe I was more man-like than I realized because, when it came to Kevin, what I saw usually trumped what he said. He saw seaweed and trash, but I saw the colorful convergence of daylight and evening. He saw an inconvenient detour to his scheduled day, but I saw the opportunity to shatter all his dull expectations.

"Just relax a little. I'm really glad we came here," I said. "The great thing about life is not knowing where a day will lead you to. Don't you think? I mean, when I woke up this morning I had no idea I would see the sun go down over the ocean."

"Technically this is the gulf," he said and squinted into the bright horizon. I knew I was making him uncomfortable, but his rigid adherence to rules and order enhanced my spontaneous spirit, and the act of pulling him away from his schedule thrilled me. "How long do you want to stay here?" he asked.

"A while."

"What does that mean? Twenty minutes? An hour?" he asked and looked down at his watch.

"Can't you just enjoy this without having a definite plan?"

"Probably not," he said and smiled.

I looked at him, thought about the Facebook *I love you* post, grabbed his hand, and said, "Just try."

Up ahead, the frame of a half-built house stood on the other side of the road, the only sign of human development along that five mile stretch of sand, but I knew what was coming. I could see the future expansion projects, the long stretches of bayous and fields filled in with buildings and crowds. Kevin was ready for the ride home, but I wanted to stare hard into those last moments of daylight when the land was still what it had always been, when the unbuilt town had still not come.

"I love you," I said but immediately knew it wasn't true.

"Why didn't you respond to my Facebook post this morning?" he asked.

"I'm telling you now," I said and searched his face for some sign of recognition.

"Are you going to write it on my Facebook wall tonight?" he asked.

"I'm telling you now. I'm telling you when it's just us, just you and me and the last traces of daylight," I said but didn't look at him. Instead my eyes studied the way the deep oranges of dusk slowly settled into the descending darkness.

"I understand," he said and kissed me mechanically.

"We should probably head back before it gets too late," I said.

"Sounds like a good plan."

*

"So he didn't say it in person?" Sam asked. It was a typical afternoon at Bayou City Café. A few scattered strangers sat at tables, mostly studying or settled into a book as they sipped their various beverages. Sam had the day off and had agreed to give me some much needed male perspective.

"No. He didn't say anything, but this morning he wrote on my Facebook page about how he had such a great time."

"Yeah, I saw that," he said. "Maybe he's just afraid of intimacy. Cassie slapped me the first time I told her I loved her.

Some people just can't deal with that stuff."

"First of all, I don't think Cassie is a good litmus test for relationship behavior. Second of all, if he's so afraid of intimacy then why is he the one initiating it over the computer?"

"I really don't have the answers to that stuff. If I did, do you think I would have gotten back together with Cassie last night?"

"You're kidding!"

"Nope. She came over at three, crawled into bed with me, scared the shit out of me, and begged me to give her another chance."

"She still has a key to your place? I thought it was really over this time," I said and shook my head.

"I'm giving her one more chance. If she screws up again, that's it."

"That's what you said before she used your house for a drug den when you were on that business trip in Albuquerque."

"I'm just so attracted to her. Seriously, I would kill my grandmother just to be able to kiss this girl. It's insane." The older woman at the table next to us subtly shook her head.

"And I came to *you* for advice?"

"Hey, that was your choice. You should really know better," he said and smiled. "Look, he obviously feels weird telling you he loves you in person for some reason, so you need to create a situation where he feels comfortable."

"I thought that's what I was doing by bringing him to the beach," I said.

"That may have felt too contrived for a guy like him. Try to think like him. How do you think he would want to say it to you?"

"Apparently over Facebook," I said.

"I mean in person."

"I know. Well ... he's a pretty traditional guy. Maybe I should try making him dinner or something."

"Yes. Now you're thinking like him. Ask him to dinner tomorrow night."

"There is, of course one slight problem with that plan. I really
don't know how to cook. I don't think grilled cheese sandwiches
or pasta out of a box would really suffice for something like this,
right?"

"No, probably not, but cooking's really not that hard. Just
find an easy recipe, and give yourself extra time."

"Okay. I think I can do this," I said.

*

The truth is I couldn't do it. I tried but failed miserably. The
chicken was extremely over-cooked, and the mushroom sauce I
made to pour over it somehow turned out so runny that the outside of the chicken was a mushy mess, while the inside texture
was tough and almost un-chewable. Kevin seemed disappointed
that the accompanying vegetables were the microwaveable variety and therefore not peeled and washed by me, and he had no
interest in the expensive ice cream I had purchased for dessert.

"At least *you* can cook," I joked in an attempt to break up
the awkward silence. At the time, I hadn't yet learned that most
southern men count cooking skills as an almost-necessary attribute
for a potential wife. In the north, my sometimes sarcastic sense of
humor and quirky beauty worked in my favor, but, maybe in the
south, I just didn't have what it took to really attract a long-term
mate.

"Let's get these dishes done," he said and grabbed my plate.

"Oh, that's okay. I'll do them tomorrow. Want to watch a
movie or something?"

"By 'tomorrow' do you mean next week?" he asked.

"I don't know. I'll do them when I do them. It's not a big
deal."

"Actually it is kind of a big deal. You really need to work on
living a more orderly life."

"My life is fine. Seriously, don't worry about the dishes. They'll
get done. I've only reached the point of no-return once with
dishes. Trust me, I learned my lesson. I know the limits now."

"Point of no-return? What the hell does that mean?" he asked.

"One time I left a pot for a few weeks without soaking it and couldn't get the gunk out of the bottom of it, but come on ... we've all done that at least once," I said.

"No, Paige. Most people don't live like this. In the navy we're taught to keep things in order, and trust me, everything runs way smoother that way."

"So just because you're in the military, you expect me to adhere to the standards you have at your job?"

"It's really for your own good. People are happier when they have schedules and goals and good hygiene practices."

"I just feel like I can't ever get past the surface of you."

"What does that mean?" he asked.

"I mean that it just feels like you're all about appearances, not about really getting deep into who I am or letting me find out who you are. I have a job too, you know, but I don't expect people to conform to my work world. I don't care that you sometimes forget the comma when you're posting stuff on Facebook or that your texts often use the wrong your or there. Just imagine if I walked around constantly correcting people's grammar. That would be annoying and debilitating."

"So I'm annoying?"

"No, I didn't mean that. Look, I like you a lot, but wouldn't you rather go to my living room and make out on the couch and let me worry about when my dishes get done?"

"Yeah, I guess I can see your point," he said.

*

"So how did it go last night?" Abby asked.

"Not the best. It turns out I suck at cooking and that sucking at cooking makes a guy want to bring a girl back to his place and watch videos of himself singing all night instead of fooling around with her in her less-than-perfect apartment."

"Seriously?"

"Yeah, and I woke up this morning to the sound of a You Tube video of Kevin's group singing. I said, 'Good morning, sweetie,' and he said, 'God, I'm awesome' and went back to watching the video of himself on his cell phone."

"Oh, wow," she said and erupted into laughter. "So I'm guessing he didn't say 'I love you'?"

"No. It's like he was more interested in me when I was a bumbling idiot. As soon as I got comfortable and started acting more like myself, he became more self-involved and less into me."

"It makes perfect sense. He likes weak women."

"Really? Is that a thing?" I asked.

"Oh yeah."

"Well then shouldn't he like the fact that I'm a weak cook?"

"Oh, that's different."

"I know. The thing is ... I've never really tried to be a good cook. I always liked the idea of a guy cooking for me, but maybe I've been too short-sighted on that. Maybe it wouldn't kill me to—"

"Paige, stop. You're just going to have to let this play out. You've only been dating the guy for a month. There's no need to completely reinvent yourself. Just relax."

"I know."

"And it would be nice if you asked me about my life once in a while," she said.

"I asked you how you're doing when I called you."

"Yeah, and then didn't wait for an answer and went right into your stuff."

"I'm sorry. You just need to yell at me when I'm being self-centered."

"That's what I'm doing," she yelled.

"Well, so how are you? How's work?"

"Work? Who cares about work? I met a guy. We had our third date last night."

"Third date? What? Why didn't you tell me about this after the first or second date?"

"I was conducting a little experiment," she said.

"On what?"

"You."

"Me?"

"Yeah, I was waiting to see how long it would take before you would genuinely show interest in my life, but I couldn't take it anymore, so I cracked, and I guess we'll never know what would have happened. I may have been engaged to Brett before you asked me anything about my life."

"Brett – huh – I don't really like that name."

"Yeah, me either, but he makes up for it."

"Yeah, it's like my mouth wants to say Brent, but the N isn't there. It's like that girl I knew in college – Manda. I always wanted to say Amanda but—"

"And somehow we're talking about you again."

"Sorry. Sorry. How did you meet him?"

"Lilly had this party, and he was there."

"Who's Lilly again?" I asked.

"Oh, my gosh! I think I've told you twenty times. She's the court administrator I sometimes have lunch with."

"Oh, gotcha. I remember now." I didn't. "You know how I am; it's hard for me to remember names if I haven't seen the person. This whole separate worlds thing we have going on is too complicated. You should just move to Texas."

"Ha! I am not taking the bar exam again!"

"I know."

"So a bunch of us decided it would be funny to break into Lilly's friend, Mark's, house, because he was out of town, and move his furniture around."

"So when lawyers and court employees have a party they break the law?"

"There was alcohol involved," she said.

"I figured."

"So we had a blast, and Brett and I were put on bedroom duty."

"Interesting."

"Yeah, it turns out we work really well together."

"Moving bedroom furniture around ... isn't that usually reserved for a year into marriage when deep-seated resentments have already taken root and agreeing where to put the damn dresser is a nearly impossible task?" I asked.

"So they say, but it's so much more fun on a first date."

"And in someone else's house."

"Exactly!"

"So did moving around furniture inspire him to kiss you?"

"It was probably more the beer than the act of moving furniture, but yes." As she talked, I casually turned on my computer. "It's a really good situation. He's Lilly's neighbor and works as an art instructor at the community college, so things won't be weird at work with us dating." I signed into my Facebook account, saw under my notifications that Kevin had written on my wall, clicked on the notification, and there it was – *I'm sorry, Paige. I can't date you anymore. We're just too different.* My face went hot. "And he's exactly my type too – a little on the short side and fairly stocky." The post had appeared on my wall fifty minutes earlier, an eternity in the world of social media. "And the kiss ... it was one of the best of my life ... one of those kisses that makes your body go hot and—" I felt sweat beading on my forehead as I mentally spun through the rolodex of Facebook friends I had and calculated the level of humiliation Kevin's post had created for me. "It's just so crazy how everything changes so quickly. Two weeks ago I still thought about Judd all the time, and now I don't even care that he's engaged. It's just so—"

I could barely hear her as I clicked the box to delete the post. She was right. I was an awful, self-centered friend who had witnessed the radiating pain she endured a year before when her almost-fiancé abruptly ended the relationship and quickly moved on to another girl. Her new-found happiness should have overshadowed my ridiculous end to a far-from-ideal five week relationship, but it didn't. "Abby," I blurted out with a shaking voice.

"I know – you think we're moving too fast, that I shouldn't be so excited at this point. My mom said the same thing, but I really like him, and it's different than Judd. We're just having fun and letting all the emotional stuff come later."

"No. Kevin broke—"

"Seriously?" she interrupted me. "I can't talk about my life for more than five minutes without you—"

"Kevin broke up with me over Facebook," I blurted out quickly.

"Oh," she said, and there was silence on the line for a moment. "Oh," she said again and burst into laughter. "Really?"

"Really."

"And that's how you found out? Over Facebook?" she asked and started to laugh again.

"Yeah. Okay, let's go back to talking about your life now," I said.

"No, that's okay. I'm good with this. So did he change his status back to single? Is that how you found out?"

"It's worse than that," I said.

"Okay—"

"He did that, but he also wrote on my wall."

"Oh, my God! He wrote you a break-up note on your Facebook wall for everyone to see?"

"Yep."

"Oh, my God! This might be the best thing that's ever happened," she said, and I felt the vibrations of her laughter against my ear.

"Well, I'm glad my misery is so entertaining to you."

"Oh, come on. You're not miserable. You're mildly embarrassed, but you knew this guy wasn't the one, and just think about the mileage you can get out of a story like this. Did you delete the post?"

"Of course."

"How long was it on there?" she asked.

"Almost an hour."

"You'll be fine. Just go do something fun today and leave this behind you. Take a drive somewhere or meet Sam for coffee."

"You're right," I said and turned off my computer.

*

I saw Kevin about a year later. It was the first day of fall, and I sat silently in a corner booth surrounded by some friends at a bar downtown. The smoke and subtle lighting and friends' voices surrounded me as a blues band played familiar songs. Suddenly there he was, ordering confidently at the bar, unaware of my eyes tunneling through the empty expanses of open tables and onto the body I had once known. A year of living had made him more handsome, and I wanted to at least say hello, but I just sat there. As the music on stage and the conversation at the table blended together, Kevin looked over at me, and for a moment, I was back in his room on those late nights when we were far out at sea, those nights when the tapestry above the bed waved in the wind of our midnight movements and the blue carpet cradled the boat that sailed us through the hours until daybreak. I smiled at him awkwardly, that man I had almost loved. He nodded in my direction, turned away to grab his drink from the bartender, and then he was gone, and I was with my friends again, safely back on dry land.

Chapter Eight: Jeff

In a region where it was common to get married right after high school and have a few kids before twenty-five, still-single men in their late twenties were often overly eager to tie the knot. For some of those men, marriage was no longer about finding the right one; it was just about finding the willing one.

When I walked into the Xpress Lube on a fog and smog filled Saturday, the smile on the manager's face perked me up a little. "Hey, red! Long time no see. What can I do ya for?" he hollered.

"Just need an oil change," I said and handed over the keys. "Oh—and the windows don't work, so don't try to roll them down … it's kind of a piece of junk."

I shrugged apologetically, and he said, "Yeah, I remember. Maroon Buick, right?" I was confused. I hadn't had my oil changed in over six months. Was my car really so bad that it stood out among all the cars a lube shop saw in half a year?

"Yep, that's my boy," I said.

"I shoulda pinned you for one of the people who names their cars. You seem the type."

"Well, I've known him a lot longer than I've known anyone in Beaumont, so I thought he deserved a name."

"And what is it?"

"Change his oil, and maybe I'll tell you," I said. He smiled again, and I noticed that below his dirty hat and behind the grime-filled creases on the side of his face, he had kind eyes. After years

of unpleasant experiences with auto mechanics, I had come to
see them as the enemy. I always felt stupid around mechanics
as they spoke of carburetors and transmission fluid and hoses. It
was as though they were speaking another language, and I felt as
helpless as my students did when they were handed back another
essay with red marks all over their writing. I never looked at a
mechanic's name tag but instead just labeled the person as one
whose job it was to search for practically insignificant issues with
my car and charge me money.

"Deal," he said, winked, and disappeared into the garage.

After about twenty minutes, he was back, wearing that nervous facial expression I had come to loathe on mechanics because it always preceded an apologetic-sounding speech about
what was wrong with my car and how much extra it was going
to cost me. "What's wrong?" I asked.

"This is kind of hard to say. I actually waited out there for a
couple of minutes to try to muster up some courage to say it." I
dug my thumbnail into my middle finger and tried to remember
how much money I had in my checking account. "The thing is
... I remember the last time you came in here, and I told myself
that if you ever came in again that I would just do it ... that I
wouldn't be stupid twice ... that I would ask you for your number
or something ... that I would ask you on a date."

I'm not sure if I wanted to go out with him or if I was just so
relieved to not receive the news of a crucial and expensive repair.
"Oh, sure," I said.

"Oh, good ... good ... I'm so glad because I actually have
your number. It's in the system, and I was planning to call in a
few days and give it another pitch if it didn't go over this time,
but I'm so glad you agreed on the first try." He took off his hat,
pulled a clean white handkerchief out of his pocket, wiped the
sweat beads off his dirty forehead, stuffed the handkerchief back
in his pocket, held out his hand, and said, "I'm Jeff."

*

"So what's going on with the guy?" I asked Abby on the phone that evening.

"You don't remember his name, do you?"

"I'm sorry. You know I'm bad with names if I haven't met someone. Remember when you were in law school? I could never keep all those people straight. They were all just a mess of names in my head ... Chris and Donald and Kelsey and Laramie ... I have no clue who is who."

"There was no one named Laramie! We've been over this," she half shouted into the phone.

"I know. I'm just messing with you, but seriously, I need to meet people to keep them straight."

"I know."

"So how are things going with—?"

"Brett."

"With Brett?"

"Meh," she said.

"Meh?"

"Yeah, it's not the best."

"What happened?"

"The same thing that always happens," she said and sighed into the phone.

"He's not actually single?"

"No, the other thing."

"You told him you love him?"

"Yeah."

"Oh shit. You've only been dating a few weeks," I said.

"I know."

"How did it happen? What did he do?"

"I really don't want to talk about this," she said.

"And this is why I never ask you anything. You don't want to talk when I do."

"I'm just so pissed at myself right now. Why do I always do this?"

"Maybe that's what we need to figure out. Maybe if you know why you do it, you won't do it anymore."

"I know why I do it."

"You just said you didn't."

"Well, I do. It's pretty obvious why I do it."

"Why?"

"Because I'm impatient. I just want to skip all the waiting crap – the two years of dating, the constant stress about whether or not it will work out, the year long wait if it does actually work out and he does actually propose, all the stress during the wedding planning of worrying that it still won't happen. How do people deal with all of this? What happens if I waste three years of my life on a guy, and the whole thing folds at the last second? I just want to meet a guy, like him, and get married right away. I can't handle all the variables along the way."

"I know, but that's not how it works. You have to at least act like you're patient. Otherwise, you're just going to scare everyone away."

"But there has to be a guy somewhere who would be up for the get-married-right-away plan," she said.

"Let me know when you find that guy. So what happened this time?"

"We were picking up dinner at the McDonalds drive-thru, and—"

"Really? You said it at the McDonalds drive-thru? That's about the least romantic scenario imaginable," I said, cutting her off.

"Are you going to let me finish?"

"Sorry."

"So I looked over at him as he handed me a straw for my shake, and I noticed he had removed the straw wrapper for me. I thought it was so sweet and conscientious that I blurted out, 'Thanks for dinner. You're so much fun to be around. That's why I love you' ... something like that."

"You said 'I love you' because a guy took the wrapper off a straw?"

"I told you; I'm impatient, but it was more than that. That little gesture made me flash forward thirty years, and I could really see myself being happy with him."

"I know they say it's the little things that matter, but I think you might be taking that too far. I mean, we could look at this from the opposite side of things. Doesn't this guy have a decent job? Doesn't he make okay money?"

"Yeah."

"And isn't this the first time you saw him this week?"

"Yeah."

"Then what the hell is he doing taking you to the McDonalds drive-thru for a date?"

"He just wanted to do something low key," she said.

"Low-key is for after the saying of the 'I love you.' The first part of a relationship should be a little more scripted than that. Like the guy I'm going out with this weekend – he's taking me out to dinner and a movie after."

"You have a date this weekend? With who?"

"Some guy I met at the place I get my car's oil changed."

"Nice."

"So what did Brett say when you told him you love him?"

She paused for a moment and said, "He didn't really say anything. He started readjusting his rearview mirror, like there's any way it was actually in the wrong position, and then he started critiquing the road maintenance in Willmar."

"That's not good. So he didn't even acknowledge the 'I love you'?"

"Nope, and he hasn't called me since."

"What about the rest of the night? How did he act?"

"Well, we went back to my apartment to eat and watch a movie, and we watched the entire movie without saying anything to each other. After the movie, he mumbled something about being really tired, gave me a quick kiss, and basically ran out of there."

"I'm really sorry," I said. "At least you didn't say it on Face-book, right?"

"Yeah, I guess, so tell me about this guy."

*

Before I fully pulled my Buick into a parking spot in front of Chili's, I spotted my date speed-walking toward my car, holding a bouquet of roses and one of those heart-shaped boxes of choco-lates usually only seen during Valentine's season. I opened the door and said, "Wow, you didn't have to bring me anything."

He handed me the loot and said, "I debated about a teddy bear but decided against it. Sorry. I didn't want to freak you out ... too much."

I didn't know what to say, so I just smiled.

"Do you like booths or tables? Do you want to sit outside? I think they have a little patio area. It's nice today, but some people don't really like sitting outside because of bugs and stuff. Sorry, I shouldn't bring up bugs right before we eat. Granted, in some countries they actually eat bugs, so then it wouldn't really be a big deal there, but we're not in one of those countries. This is Texas ... not that I'm calling Texas a country. I ain't one of those people," he said, and any nerves I had on the drive over were gone. His obvious nervousness had a calming effect on me, and I walked with a sense of confidence toward the restaurant, staying a little ahead of my date.

He seemed different than he had in the lube shop, out of his element and less attractive. I had assumed he would move up on the attractiveness ladder a bit after a shower and clean clothes, but the opposite had happened. Without the dirt and coveralls, Jeff looked like a tall, slightly chubby kid with wrinkles around his eyes and on his forehead. He wore pleated black pants and a teal colored shirt tucked in, a wardrobe decision that wasn't flattering on his husky frame. As he stepped ahead of me and held the lobby door open, my nose was attacked by his rookie mistake of over-applying cologne.

"So booth or table?" he asked me as we approached the hostess station.

"Booth works for me," I said, and the hostess nodded.

"So what are you doing tomorrow morning at 10:30?" he asked as I scooted into the booth.

"Sleeping, why?"

"I told my mom I would see if you could come to church with us. She'd really like to meet you," he said, and I looked down at my menu, hoping that when I looked back up, he would magically be gone.

"Maybe next week ... I'll let you know."

"I hear you. I hear you. Look, I just want you to know that I'm a really nice guy. I can tell for sure that you're a nice person and that you're the kind of girl I've been looking for, but I wanted you to know that I would always be nice to you. It's just who I am. I make 37,000 a year at my job. I know that's not much, but I have other ideas in the works. I actually applied for a couple of higher paying jobs this week." There he was, talking about being a good potential husband for me, and I was contemplating faking sudden stomach spasms and rushing out of there.

"Well, that's good."

"And I have stuff—good stuff." I thought he might be talking about marijuana, but he went on. "I have a huge flat screen TV, a treadmill and weights, a nice queen-sized bed , and a brand new leather sofa, and if you're a really good girl, all that could be yours."

"Sounds good," I said lifelessly and decided to order the club sandwich.

The waitress came over to take our order. Jeff looked at her nametag and kept using her name while he ordered, an unnatural attempt at familiarity that seemed to annoy her the same way it had annoyed me when I waited tables in high school.

"I'm so glad this is all working out," Jeff said after our waitress left the table. "You're going to really like my place. It's the opposite of my work – everything is all very clean and organized. You should come over after the movie. We could watch a second movie at my place. I have almost everything. In fact, if you want to skip the formality of sitting in a movie theater chair, we could just watch a movie or two at my place instead."

Images of being tied up against my will or violently raped on his kitchen floor flooded my mind, but even the thought of cuddling with this guy on his couch was repellent. I had entered the date with only marginal interest, and his idealistic certainty that this date would lead to a lifelong relationship horrified me. I had heard accounts of couples that met and married almost immediately and could even imagine myself in such a scenario, meeting a man whose appearance and characteristics convinced me that no one better could exist, but Jeff was not this man. "I think we should go to the theater this time. I like to know people better before I visit their apartment," I said.

"You're smart. I like that. It's one of the many things I really admire about you," he said.

"You don't really know anything about me."

"I know enough."

"We just had that short conversation at the shop and an even shorter conversation on the phone. All you really know is that I drive a Buick, look like this, and enjoy a club sandwich."

"Yes, but I also know that you're too cautious to go over to a guy's place on a first date, so that's good, and I know that you're an English teacher, which means you're educated and driven and all that."

"Wait—how do you know I'm a teacher? I don't remember telling you that."

"I looked you up."

"You googled me?" I asked.

"Yeah. I found out all sorts of cool stuff about you." Jeff had just broken an important dating rule. He had openly admitted to internet stalking. It's true that the practice of using the internet to research a stranger's life had become so popular in the culture that it was almost expected, and many people use this tool to sort out potential mates from complete disasters. Still, those of us, like myself, who had started dating before the internet fully bloomed still held internet stalking at a level of creepiness that was not completely separate from the idea of a man obtaining the same information by peeping in a woman's windows or following her around town. We knew internet stalking happened, even engaged in it ourselves from time to time, but we didn't enjoy the image of a man at home in his underwear, staring at a computer screen with wide eyes at the details of our lives. "Did you look me up?" he asked and looked at me with hopeful eyes.

"No, I can't say I did."

"Weren't you curious?"

"I like to just go into these things with a clear mind," I said and took a sip of my soda. At that point, I already knew there was no way Jeff could turn the date around. Some people claim that a woman knows whether or not she is interested in a man within the first thirty seconds of a date. For me, it wasn't quite so extreme, but there were certain mistakes that could instantly derail any possibility of wanting to see a guy again, and when Jeff asked me to meet his mother at church the next morning, the train didn't just veer off the tracks; it exploded into flames.

"So what do you do for fun? I couldn't find that online," he said and chuckled nervously.

"I like bowling and table tennis."

"That's perfect. My apartment is close to Saturn Bowl, and my parents have a ping pong table in their garage. If you're not doing anything tomorrow afternoon, you should come over and hang out. My mom usually makes gumbo on Sundays."

"I really can't tomorrow. I have a lot of work to do."

"Well, maybe some night this week would work for you. What nights are you free?"

"I don't really know yet. I'll call you when I have my work schedule."

"That works. When do you think you'll call?"

"I'll try to call sometime early this week."

"You know, if you have a lot of work to do tomorrow, I could hang out with you while you work. I could make you lunch. You have to eat, right?"

"That's really a nice offer, but I should probably just get my work done tomorrow."

"Or we could go out somewhere, if you're feeling weird about being alone with me ... because I totally get that, if that's the case, and we could go get fast food if you're on a major time crunch, maybe eat in a park somewhere. You could work outside. Doesn't that sound fun?"

"I really appreciate the offer," I said as the waitress dropped off our food. "But I do need a day to myself tomorrow. I'm kind of a loner sometimes. I like to have a few days to myself every week."

"I respect that," he said. "I guess I just wanted to have a chance to show off my cooking skills and to show you that my place is super clean. To be honest, when we're together I wouldn't mind cooking for you on a regular basis. Hell, I don't even mind cleaning. I would gladly do your laundry or vacuum your place when you have a lot of work to do. I just want to be around you," he said. I didn't want Jeff to be my boyfriend, but he momentarily sparked my interest with the idea of having a free servant.

"That's really not necessary. I don't mind doing that stuff myself," I said.

"And obviously I'm good at fixing cars, so you wouldn't have to worry about that." I looked up from my sandwich and smiled. "And I'm really good at backrubs." As he continued to make more promises, I realized my approach to relationships may have been all wrong. Maybe dating was like buying a car, the longer you held out, the more the negotiation moved in your favor.

"Cool."

"And I like to travel. I could see us driving down to Galveston a lot or over to New Orleans, if you like jazz."

"I do."

"God, I knew I had found something special the first time I saw you," he said. "It really feels like those stories you hear where people just know." I wondered if the woman usually felt my intense pang of nausea in those stories.

"We're just getting to know each other. Relax a little."

"I'll try," he said and picked up his fork for the first time.

Jeff watched me as I chewed my sandwich, watched me as I sipped my cherry coke, watched as I dipped fries in the mound of ketchup on the side of my plate, and watched as I surveyed the activity in the parking lot beyond the window in an attempt to avoid his silent request for eye contact. In my vision's periphery, I noticed that, with all his watching of me, Jeff wasn't eating his dinner, and, by the time I had inhaled all the contents of my plate, he had only managed to nibble the edges of his pile of mashed potatoes. "Are you feeling okay?" I asked.

"Yeah, great. You?"

"Yeah, I feel fine. I meant because you're not eating," I said.

"Oh, well ... to be honest, I'm a little too nervous to eat. I've just been looking forward to this for so long."

"We just met a couple of days ago."

"I know. I know. I guess I meant it as more than this date. You know what I mean? Like, I've been looking forward to you, I guess you could say."

I looked at his untouched steak and forced a smile. As he waved the waitress over to retrieve the check, I wondered how Abby would react to a guy like Jeff. Would his eagerness send them racing to the nearest courthouse, or were we all naturally suspicious of the love-at-first-sight concept when we were on the receiving end of the idea?

"Would you like a box for that?" the waitress asked, pointing to the twelve dollar steak.

"Nah, we're going to a movie, so it'd just go bad in the car," he said.

"Oh, okay," she said with confusion in her voice. "Maybe you shoulda just ordered a fourth of a serving of mashed potatoes or six kernels of corn ... woulda saved you some cash."

"Oh, no big deal. I'm just happy to help out the restaurant," he said.

"I'm sorry," I said as she walked away.

"Nah, don't worry. This is the most fun I've ever had wasting food."

"I think my most fun food-wasting experience was this time at McDonalds when the guy making my burger kept wiping his runny nose on his sleeve and then sneezed several times into his gloved hands and didn't bother to change the gloves afterwards. I just paid for my food, took the bag of food, and threw it in the trash on the way out of the restaurant."

"See – you lost your appetite. I'm just too mesmerized to care about mine," he said and handed the waitress his credit card.

Outside of the restaurant, Jeff walked a step behind me and placed his hand on my lower back, a gesture that must have looked more like an officer leading a prisoner into his cell than a man on a date with a woman. "I'll follow you over there," he said when we got to my car.

"Or I could follow you."

"No, I'll follow you over," he insisted.

I considered the options, pictured myself speeding out of the parking lot, down the street, running red lights, whipping unexpectedly around corners, escaping from Jeff's view, and getting home to my empty apartment. As Jeff casually walked to his truck, I put the key in the ignition and shifted the car into drive, but I caught a glimpse of the flowers and chocolates in the back seat and knew I couldn't do it, couldn't ditch my date at the midway point and leave him wondering what went wrong. I thought of Abby and my high school self, waited for Jeff's white truck to pull out of its parking spot, and slowly exited the lot.

*

"You have to meet the manager," Jeff said to me after buying tickets to *The Curious Case of Benjamin Button.* "He's a really good guy. We went to high school together."

"Okay."

"To be honest, I usually get free tickets from him, but I didn't want you to think I was cheap."

"Oh, no. That would have been fine."

He grabbed my hand, and I held on loosely as we moved through the crowd of people waiting for snacks and sodas. Back behind the concession stand, the manager's little office betrayed the ambiance of the rest of the theater. It was like walking into the dirty kitchen of a five-star restaurant. The manager's office, with its paint-peeling walls and its ugly orange metal table and its old shelves stacked high with dusty file folders and its dingy moss green carpet, had obviously been neglected during the many re-models since the theater opened. A large bald man, who appeared to be sweating more than my date, extended his arms and pulled me in for an aggressively-friendly bear hug. "It's so good to meet you, Paige. Wow, I've heard so much about you!" *Heard so much about me?* I had just met Jeff. How could this guy have heard anything about me?

"Thanks. Nice to meet you too."

"It's like I told Jeff here – when you know, you know. When I met Elsie, I knew right away," he said and pointed to a gold wedding band.

"Oh, we're just on a first date," I said, shaking my head.

"Well, you'll be surprised how fast it goes. You'll blink twice and be celebrating your kid's first birthday," this manager said, and I noticed Jeff's face was beaming. Suddenly the stale air in that musty office strangled my ability to take a full breath, and I felt my legs weakening beneath me. I leaned into Jeff's sturdy body for support, a gesture he unfortunately mistook for affection rather than intense fear. I didn't want to blink twice and be the photo of a wife in a crummy little office somewhere. I had to get out of there, back outside where I could breathe.

"Ready for the show, darlin'?" Jeff asked me.

"Sure."

We walked to our seats and settled in. I noticed there were only a few other people in the theater, a fact that disappointed me but seemed to delight Jeff. "Looks like we've pretty much got the place to ourselves," he said and squeezed my arm. I folded my hands and placed them on my left leg and away from Jeff, an uncomfortable sitting position but a much needed attempt to avoid any movie cuddling. The previews began, and, as soon as a bride and groom appeared on the screen in a preview for *Bride Wars*, Jeff leaned in close and said softly, "That could be us." I leaned away a little, bit my lower lip, and sighed audibly, knowing the two hour movie would feel much longer.

Despite my best efforts, there was no way to avoid contact during the show. Jeff fished my hand out of my lap, held it a little too tightly, and placed his free arm around me. Because I didn't want the couple at the end of our row to be distracted from the show, I resisted the urge to fight off Jeff's physical advances and just sat there while he alternated between putting his arm around me and petting me from elbow to wrist. My passive attitude lasted about thirty minutes into the show but abruptly ended when Jeff's hand landed on my knee and began moving up. "Hey," I shout-whispered, calling attention to my disaster of a date. He retreated, but it didn't take long for the whole process to begin again.

As we traveled deeper into the plot of the movie and my shoes stuck harder to the soda stained floor and Jeff's attempts to touch my thigh were happening at closer and closer intervals, I began to strategize ways to avoid the goodnight kiss I knew Jeff would attempt later, out by my car in the dark parking lot. There were a lot of ways to dodge a kiss. I could put on an air of aloof disinterest on my walk to the car, but it was clear that a guy like Jeff would fail to pick up on any signals. I could be honest and express my lack of interest openly, but that kind of awkwardness seemed unfair to both of us. I could turn my head a little when he went in for the kiss, but Jeff was obviously persistent enough to nuzzle his eager mouth into mine and overcome my attempt to avoid it. It seemed the only real option was to tell Jeff I had a wait-until-the-second-date-to-kiss rule.

Jeff's hand landed on my knee again, and I pushed it away again, and up on the screen one of the characters said," He loved you from the first time he saw you."

Jeff leaned in and whispered to me, "I know the feeling."

I wanted out. What did this guy think was happening? Did he really believe that we were falling in love after a couple of dull conversations, a dinner at Chili's, and a few one-sided embraces? Maybe I should have just stood up right then, rushed out of there, and sprinted to my old Buick, but I stayed. Social conventions forbid that kind of escape, but after his comment about falling in love with me, I grabbed my purse and put a little Chap Stick on my lips, and I held the purse in my lap for the rest of the show so I could get out quickly if I felt I had to.

As the emotional peaks of the movie played out on the screen, I noticed in my peripheral vision that Jeff was crying. I had been so preoccupied by the intense cloud of cologne enveloping me and by the constant chore of wriggling out of Jeff's groping hands that my mind never made the leap from what was happening in my seat to what the characters were feeling on the screen. I looked over at the couple down the row from us, saw the woman wiping her face with a tissue and her date affectionately rubbing her shoulder, and suddenly everything seemed funny, and the fact that people around me were crying made it all even funnier. I thought about how I would have to find another place to take my car for repairs and oil changes, and I thought about Jeff's mom ironing a church dress to meet her son's future wife in. I thought about Jeff's uneaten steak and the chocolates melting into a messy glob in the backseat of my car and Jeff telling his friends that I was the one, and I couldn't hold it in anymore. There in the theater, as the music and images on screen pained the hearts of those around me, I started to laugh. I covered my mouth with my hand and bit down hard on the skin across my palm to try to stop it, but it didn't help. My whole body shook, and the laughter erupted through my covered mouth and out into the theater. Jeff shot me a confused look, and the woman down the row assertively shushed me. "Why are you laughing?" Jeff whispered.

"I don't know. I'm sorry," I managed through giggles.

"Let's get out of here," he said.

I nodded and stood up, happy to be a few minutes ahead of schedule and closer to the conclusion of the date. "I'm really sorry," I said out in the hallway. "I don't know what happened. I guess it just seemed ludicrous to me that such a ridiculous premise brought people to tears."

"You didn't like the movie?"

"It's not that. It was good. I just couldn't get sad about it. Sorry."

"Don't be. I like that about you," he said and stopped walking. "I really feel good about this. The thing is ... I need someone like you, you know? I knew that the first time I saw you. There's something about you that complements the way I am. I'm a mechanic, and you're reading books and stuff. You were reading some book the first time you came in, back a few months ago, and I said to myself, 'If that girl comes in here again, I'm going to do something about it, really make it happen.' And I like that you laugh at sad movies. I mean, who does that? Right? I just really see this working out." I didn't make eye contact with him while he talked, so I didn't notice until the last second that he had stepped in and started to lean down for a kiss. I stepped back to avoid him, lost my balance, and fell down onto the dirty maroon carpet. "You okay?" he asked and reached out a hand to help me up.

I shook my head to deny his hand and instead situated myself in a more comfortable position, sitting down with my legs out in front of me, holding the back of my knees in my hands right there in the middle of that theater hallway. "I'm fine. I just don't want to kiss you," I said and was possibly more surprised than he was at my blunt response.

"Oh. Did I do something?" he asked.

I looked up at him and down at my knees and said, "No. You're fine. I just don't see this happening."

"So we're not going to keep going out?"

"No, I don't think so," I said and pushed myself back up to a standing position.

"Are you sure?"

"Yeah."

"Oh," he said and stood there for a moment, staring back at the theater door, maybe considering watching the last few minutes of the film. "Okay," he said, turned around quickly, and started speed walking ahead of me and toward the exit. I thought about trying to catch up to him, to say something more, but there really wasn't anything more to say, so instead I walked slowly and watched as his back disappeared around the corner and out into the empty lobby.

In Jeff's hopeful version of the evening, we left the theater together, holding hands and walking leisurely to the parking lot, but in the reality I created, I held my own hand on the way out of the theater. In a way I was always doing that, always holding the hand of my future self, trying to be cognizant of her needs and desires, trying to walk through life in such a way that her future footsteps would be easier to bear.

*

Back at home that night I stared hard into my bedroom mirror, trying to see myself as I was at twenty-nine, trying to hold the image and preserve it in the deep tunnels of memory, trying to stare hard at the flicker of my gaze and the smooth slope of my nose to remember it and to also resurrect the forgotten hours of my life. I thought about my parents and how they met at nineteen, how they had someone who would see them in the old years and remember them in the very young. I stared at my face and understood that I wasn't going to have that, that the men who knew me at sixteen, at nineteen, at twenty-two wouldn't be there to still see that searching girl when the clock ticked over to her last year.

I knew I could tell a man someday about how the winds howled hard over the wide expanses of the prairie where I lived during college, about how awful my hair looked after I dyed it black junior year of high school, about the way my grandfather's voice had light in it as he told the old stories on dark winter nights in a house full of relatives. I could see my future spouse sitting there, listening to me struggle to bring the old pieces of my life back into the room; but I understood that he would only ever see these things second-hand, and that's why I stared so hard at myself. I knew I would have to remember it all, to remember it all alone.

*

At the beginning of 2009, Sam and I found ourselves in a crowded bar in downtown Beaumont. It was one of those days that felt cold in Texas but would have been considered mild by Minnesota standards. Temperatures hovered around fifty, and a light rain fell outside. Sam had just caught Cassie getting a lap dance at the strip club near her apartment, and he needed a few drinks and someone to listen to him rant a little.

"So I'm confused," I said. "I thought you didn't like strip clubs."

"I don't. I saw her car in the parking lot and freaked out a little. I thought maybe she was working there behind my back, so I went in to check it out."

"Really?" I said with raised eyebrows.

"Seriously. Come on, you've seen her car. No one else in the world has a pink hatchback with an orange bumper and white wings painted on the sides."

"True ... so you saw her car and decided to go in—"

"Yeah, and there she was, getting a lap dance from an overweight stripper. I seriously can't get the image of black back fat out of my head."

"So what did she say when you confronted her?"

"She kind of flipped out at me."

"*She* flipped out at *you*?"

"Yeah. She said it was just something she wanted to do since she hadn't ever done it before, said I was overreacting." He took a sip of his beer. "Maybe I am overreacting."

"I don't think so, and it's not like this is an isolated incident, and whatever happened to people telling each other everything when they're dating? At the very least you could say she wasn't honest with you."

"There are a lot of things that I keep from Cassie. People don't need to tell each other everything."

"Like what? What do you keep from her?" I asked.

He took another swig of beer and said, "She doesn't know I shave the hair off my knuckles or that I'm sometimes in such a rush getting ready for work that I pee while brushing my teeth."

"First of all, gross. And second of all, that's not the same thing. Look, didn't you say you had plans with Cassie that night? Isn't that why you drove by the strip club?"

"Yeah."

"So this is obviously another one of her attempts to freak you out, to cause drama, to avoid getting too close to you. I just think you're wasting your time with her. I mean, imagine what she would do if you ever tried to propose. She'd probably start your car on fire or try to sleep with your dad."

"I know. I know. I just can't stop, though," he said while pushing the rounded bottom of his beer glass into the old wood table. "Everything else is so boring. Look at this." He nodded in the direction of the crowd waiting at the bar for a new drink. "I don't want to date any of these people. I want Cassie. I can see her eyes in the dark when we're in bed together. I can see her body and her full lips before she even walks into a room. I don't want any of these women. What the hell am I gonna do?"

"I don't know."

"I have to end it. You're right. Cold turkey, whatever the heck that phrase even means."

I pushed up the sleeves of my yellow sweater, looked over at the door, and there he was – Jeff, wearing his work coveralls and accompanied by a few men who also worked at the shop. Knowing my long red hair and bright yellow top offered little chance of anonymity, I smiled straight at him and waved him over to say hello. He broke away from his friends, walked up to my table, and said, "What?"

"Hey. I just wanted to say hi. It's nice to see you. How've you been?"

"Well ... I'd be a hell of a lot better if some bitch didn't break my heart," he said.

I looked over at Sam, not sure what to say or what to do, hoping he would do something, but he was taken as much off guard as I was. "Okay," I said and nodded curtly with pursed lips. "Never mind." Jeff walked away and back to his friends, and I said to Sam, "That reminds me. I need to get my oil changed this week."

Sam laughed and said, "Who the heck was that?"

"*That* was that mechanic guy I went out with once, like half a year ago."

He laughed again and said, "Didn't you just go on one date?"

"Yeah!"

"Weird. Do you think he's already drunk?"

"I don't know," I said and watched as Jeff grabbed a glass from the pretty bartender and headed to a table in close proximity to where Sam and I sat. "I'm kind of tired. I think I might call it a night."

"Because of that?" he said, pointing to Jeff.

"No," I lied. "I'm just tired. Do you mind?"

"No, it's okay. Want me to walk you out?" he asked.

"No, I can make it. Go ahead and finish that up," I said and nodded at his unfinished mug of beer.

"Do you want to take my umbrella?"

"No thanks. I think I heard someone say the rain stopped."

"Oh, okay. I'll keep an eye on that guy and make sure he doesn't follow you out."

"Thanks."

"So, compared to that, maybe Cassie's not all that crazy," he said.

"Yeah, maybe not," I said, not having enough energy to reopen the Cassie conversation.

*

I thought about calling Abby on the way home but instead just drove, and I found myself watching what was happening beyond the road more than the road itself. Beaumont at midnight became the kind of place where a woman didn't want to run out of gas or even linger at a stop light too long. I didn't want to be afraid of the people who staggered slowly down the dark streets and seemed to be heading in no particular direction, but I was. I passed The Palace Motel, an old single-story building with a cracked-concrete parking lot, a weather-beaten roof, and a sign out front that read SHIRTS REQUIRED. A couple of men stood beside the bushes in front of the motel, cigarettes in hand and blowing streams of smoke out into the black night. I found myself looking down again and again at the lock to reassure myself that I was safely separated from these strangers by the boundaries of my car.

I passed Avenue A and watched a slump-shouldered woman push a stroller along the edge of the street, I drove another block and saw a circle of young men shouting at each other, and I almost made eye contact with the bearded man perched on the incline under the freeway overpass. What had I been complaining about? I didn't have a boyfriend, but these people, people of my city, people all around me, didn't seem to have anything. I felt like a fool, pointing out my life's one little deficiency and giving it all my attention.

Still, I couldn't help myself. I had spent so many years filling in the blank spaces of who I am, and I knew my face and ideas and dreams and could travel confidently on most roads that twisted and intersected on the map of myself. This was why sometimes I wanted to leave the places I had invented, drive out past the streams and towns and mileposts of my own mind. This is why I wanted to keep driving, out beyond the edges of myself and onto the map of another's mind. This is why I wanted to fall in love.

Chapter Nine: Adam

In February of 2009, I was about three months into my six-month membership with an online dating site when I began to solicit friends for advice on how to get better results.

"Don't date online. Everyone on there is a creep, is married and using online dating as a way to cheat, or has no social skills," one friend said, but I was too optimistic to buy into that theory.

"Talk to a guy for a while before agreeing to meet in person," said someone else, but that plan had backfired for my friend, Sara.

"My friends, Joe and Janine, met online, and they're happily married now," said a supportive coworker, but these friends she referred to lived in Houston, a city that was often listed among the ten best places in America for young singles. Houston housed four million people, was a center for international business, offered some of the best medical facilities in Texas, and featured a thriving and varied array of nightlife activities. Beaumont, though only ninety miles from Houston, had little in common with its much bigger and more popular brother city. I often imagined beautiful Houstonites sipping martinis at Shay's Downtown Lounge while I spent another Saturday at home or out with coworkers at a place called Scramblin' Mike's, a bar that offered two dollar beers and a chance to see the same twenty people who were always there. I knew that a Houston guy would have no interest in driving an hour and a half each way for a date when he had a whole city filled with prospects and over a hundred women his age to choose from right there on the dating site. Still, on late nights, when I couldn't sleep, I sometimes recreationally perused the dozens of pages of Houston guys looking for their match. Occasionally I even emailed one, but usually I never received a message back or got a quick explanation about how far the drive was or how pointless it would be to start something that could potentially become complicated.

Sam offered more practical advice. "Make the date short – the shorter the better," he said. "Try to encourage guys to meet you at a coffee shop. That way you can control how long things go. If you like him, sip slowly. You can make a cup of coffee last hours with strategic sipping. If you don't like him, gulp it down and get out of there," he said while sipping his cocoa and surveying the coffee shop for potential dates.

*

It didn't take long for me to test out Sam's advice. I came home from work, threw my purse and book bag on the couch, grabbed a cherry coke, and rushed to the office to check my Match.com email. I had three emails in my inbox.

Email one:

> *Hey Darlin,*
>
> *I seen your pictures and wanted to say your pretty. I got a boat and maybe we could take a ride out on the Neches some time. Let me know what u think?*
>
> *Bill*

Email two:

> *Hello,*
>
> *You are receiving this email because something in your profile struck me as interesting, and I think it would be beneficial for us to get to know each other. Please check out my profile and respond if you feel the same way.*
>
> *Brett*

Email three:

> *Hi Paige,*
>
> *I really liked your profile, especially the fact that you like to travel and enjoy good food and conversation. It looks like we'd get along great. It also helps that you're a cute redhead.*
>
> *Adam*

Upon further inspection, it turned out that Email One Guy was sixty-one and had been divorced five times (a piece of information he probably should have left off his dating profile page). Email Two Guy was clearly playing by the strategy of sending out a form email to as many girls as possible and sitting back and waiting for someone to respond; but this Adam guy seemed like a good prospect. He appeared to be decently attractive in the picture he posted of himself wearing a red sweater and towering over a small Christmas tree. He had a job as a graphic designer and was only three years younger than I.

After a few emails, we agreed to meet at the Starbucks inside of Barnes and Noble at eight on a Saturday night.

I showed up right at eight and spotted him easily. He waved me over to the corner table where he sat with a coffee in hand. "I'm Paige."

"I figured," he said and shook my hand.

"I'm gonna go grab a mocha."

"Sounds good."

I didn't mind that he didn't offer to pay. At least he had bought his own drink.

I got my iced mocha, nervously sat down, and smiled at Adam.

"You actually look like your picture," he said.

"Oh, thanks. I know what you mean. I went out with this guy a few weeks ago, and there was literally no way he was the same guy as the guy in the pictures."

"So what did you do?" he asked.

"Nothing really. What could I do? I just stared at him the whole time, trying to figure out if he could possibly be the guy from the pictures."

"I think I would've flipped out," he said.

"Oh, no ... It wasn't a big deal. I just didn't go out with him again."

"Because he was ugly, right? Ugly people should seriously not try to date. It's such a waste of time, not to mention annoying."

"No. It wasn't even about that. I just didn't like the deception part of it. It felt suspicious."

"Was he ugly?" he asked.

"He wasn't very attractive, but that really wasn't the reason. Trust me; I'm not shallow."

"Bull shit!" he half shouted and looked straight at me with his dull gray eyes.

I laughed uncomfortably and said, "So you're a graphic designer?"

"Yep."

"How do you like that?"

"It's okay. At least I don't have to deal with people," he said.

"Yeah, customer service jobs can be difficult."

"Yep," he said and seemed to be staring at the Edgar Allan Poe poster behind me.

"So what made you decide to become a graphic designer?" I asked, desperate for a way to keep the conversation going.

"I worked at Toys R Us," he said.

"You mean before you were a graphic designer?"

"Yeah."

"And you didn't like Toys R Us?" I asked.

"I fucking hated that bullshit. That's why I went back to school."

"What was so bad about Toys R Us?" I asked and took a big sip of my mocha.

"I worked there before Christmas, and they had this huge fucking Santa that waved at you when you walked by. I hated that fucking thing. He had this smug look on his face," he said and curled his lips up a bit to show his revulsion.

"Okay ..."

"They kept a lot of the new toys at the front of the store ... big displays of 'em ... I had to see that Santa most of my shift because I was the new guy, and the manager didn't let me run the register, and I had to spend hours straightening those front displays. Fucking bull shit." I started drinking my mocha faster and looked around more frequently to indicate my loss of interest. He went on. "It got to the point where I felt like Santa was taunting me. Do you know what that feels like? Fucking bull shit – that's what." I nodded nervously. "I had to get rid of that damn thing, so I brought a sledge hammer to work one night when I was scheduled to close."

"You what?"

"That's right. Clever, huh?" I nodded, knowing that if this guy was capable of smashing a smiling Santa's skull in, I didn't want to piss him off. "So after my shift that night, while the manager was in the back counting the money, I got the hammer out of my coat and smashed the shit out of him."

"Seriously?"

"Yeah." He was smiling but in the evil, I-tortured-small-animals-as-a-child, kind of way. "Needless to say, my manager totally flipped out and fired me, but it was well worth it."

I aggressively sucked down more mocha, regretting my decision to order a large and wishing I hadn't chosen a drink that came in a clear cup. "You must really hate Santa," I said.

"It wasn't about that. Like I said, it was the smug way he looked at me."

"Okay ..."

"But at least that job was better than Walgreens."

"You worked at Walgreens? That was my first job," I said.

"Did you work in the photo development department?"

"No, I worked at the front register."

"Then you have no idea of the kind of hell I endured."

"Like what?"

"People act like their pictures are fucking crack or something. 'Are my pictures ready yet?' 'Are my pictures ready yet?' 'Are my pictures ready yet?' Shit drove me insane! One day I couldn't take it anymore."

"What did you do?"

"There were people everywhere. It was a Saturday, so we were running behind schedule, but those fuckers couldn't understand that. 'Are my pictures ready yet?' 'Are my pictures ready yet?'" he said in a mocking, high pitched tone. "Well, I got fed up, so I kind of flipped out."

"What happened?"

"I started tearing up their stupid pictures and walked out."

"Wow. Seriously?"

"Hell, yeah! That was right before I got the stupid job at Toys R Us," he said.

"And graphic design is working out better?" I asked.

"Oh, yeah. No comparison."

I finished the last two inches of my coffee in one gulp and said, "Well, it was really nice meeting you. Unfortunately, I have a bunch of papers to grade before tomorrow, so I'm gonna call it a night."

"Cool," he said and didn't get up fast enough to offer a handshake or hug before I bolted for the nearest trash can, tossed my cup and straw wrapper in, and headed for the door.

*

Later that night I wondered if maybe Adam's dating strategy was to act like a guy with an anger problem if he wasn't attracted to the girl from the dating site he agreed to meet. It made sense, so much sense, in fact, that I had momentarily considered using this strategy in the future if a situation got desperate enough.

This hypothesis only lasted until the next afternoon, though, when I got a text from Adam saying that he had a nice time meeting me and wanted to have dinner sometime.

I never responded.

Chapter Ten: Himesh

One of the great benefits of living in an apartment was the always-present possibility of listening in on private conversations. This seemed to be especially true in cities like Beaumont where industrial jobs were plentiful and highly-educated citizens were not. After living in my apartment for a couple of years, I understood that the frequency of these eavesdropping opportunities intensified on weekends, as the clock crept closer to midnight, and often lasted well into the final hour of darkness.

It was Saturday night again, and there was nothing to do but sit alone in my apartment. I caught myself reciting the characters' lines in unison with the actors as I watched *Serendipity* for the third time that week. It was pathetic, but I couldn't handle the silence, and something about the music and the colors and the hopeful looks on the actors' faces soothed me out of my loneliness.

Just as the scene opened up on the skating rink and the climax approached, I heard voices outside and muted my TV. "No, I didn't!" a woman yelled. "I just axed you a simple favor. Holy fucking shit! This is why you's on that couch half the nights – shit like this."

"Whatever, Keish. I'm done," a male voice responded.

"Oh, hell no, you ain't!" screamed Keish. They were down in the parking lot, so I slid the window open about an inch, and the acoustics were great. "Excuse me," she yelled. "Excuse me. I don't mean ta bother ya, but can I ax you a question?"

"Sure," replied a new man's voice.

"Would you ever carry your wife's purse?" she asked.

"She carries her own purse," new man said.

"I understand that, but if she really needed you to?" she asked.

"Well, sure. I suppose," new man said.

"See!" she yelled. "See, Don! Some men ain't so self-absorbed that they won't carry they woman's damn purse!" I bit my hand a little to stifle the desire to laugh.

"Damn it, Keish. You gotta let a man be a man. I'm done with this shit," Don shouted.

*

It was almost midnight, and the action in the parking lot had subsided surprisingly early for a Saturday, so I logged onto Facebook. It didn't take long, after I turned on the chat function, for Himesh to type, "Hello."

"Hey, I'm surprised you're up so late," I typed in, and clicked the send button.

"Why's that?"

"You said something about being on an early schedule."

"True, but I'm living outside of the box tonight," he wrote.

"Oh, really? What did you do?"

"I'm online past ten."

"Oh. Haha. I thought maybe there was more to the story," I wrote.

"Nope. That's about it."

I should have politely said goodnight and logged off. After all, this was not a friend of mine or someone I worked with. He was just a guy I had met on *Match.com* and gone on two duller-than-normal dates with. He even lived an hour away, so there was little possibility of running into him in real life. After the second date, I had decided to decline an offer for date number three if it was given, but I had forgotten to delete Himesh as a Facebook friend, a necessary step to avoid the awkwardness of him knowing about any future male-related developments in my life. "And that's the problem with you," I wrote. "That's why we didn't really hit it off."

"What do you mean?"

"You're not very much fun. You're all order and responsibility. You're not at all spontaneous." It was so much easier to write the truth than to say it. Something about not hearing a person's voice made it not quite real, so I felt safely sequestered behind the locked doors of my little apartment to write whatever I felt.

"Oh, I can be spontaneous," he wrote.

"I thought engineers didn't have that gear."

"You don't know me very well."

"Okay. What's the most spontaneous thing you've done?" I asked.

It took a few minutes for a response to come, so I went to the kitchen for a cherry coke and came back to "I bought tickets for an LSU game on eBay two days before the game and spent the night of the game at a friend's house I barely knew."

"But this was all planned out two days in advance?" I asked.

"You obviously don't know much about LSU tickets. People usually plan game trips months in advance."

"Okay, but you've never done something right on the spot?"

"No. Who does that?" he asked.

"People who are capable of spontaneity."

"I'm capable. I've just never had a real reason to do it. I get the sense that you see me as this boring guy, but that's not me. You don't really know me," he wrote.

"You can be exciting?"

"Of course."

"Okay. Prove it."

"Gladly. How do you propose I do that?" he asked.

I thought for a minute and wrote, "Come hang out with me now."

"Now? It's after midnight."

"I know. It'll be fun. We can have a totally unconventional date, and you can prove to me that you're more interesting than you seem. We can go bowling at the all night alley or go out for coffee and talk until the sun comes up. Doesn't that sound like fun?"

"You do know that Lake Charles is over an hour away, right?"

"You said you could be spontaneous, so I'm giving you something that qualifies, a chance to back up your statement."

"Okay. I'm leaving here in five minutes," he wrote. "Text me your address, and I'll see you in a little over an hour."

*

"Hey," Abby said in a slightly groggy voice. "What time is it?"

"I know I'm calling kind of late, but it's the weekend, and there's a bit of a situation," I said.

"Oh, God. What did you do?" she asked in that judgmental tone I had grown to love.

"Don't yell at me."

"I'm not awake enough to yell."

"I can't believe you were asleep. You used to stay up 'til two."

"I used to not have a real job. So tell me what's going on or I'm hanging up."

"Okay, okay—" I said and stalled for a moment. "You know that Himesh guy I met on Match?"

"Yeah—"

"Well, I accidentally invited him over."

"I thought we decided *that* was a no-go," she said.

"I know, but you know how I am about making decisions after midnight."

"So when is he coming over?"

"Now."

"Now? Doesn't he live in Louisiana?"

"I know. I don't know what happened. We were talking on Facebook, and all of a sudden I was challenging him to drive here and hang out all night," I said.

She started to laugh. "I've gotta say, I'm actually going to put this in the worth-waking-me-up-for category."

"Really? I can't believe it made the cut. I mean, we all know death and major illness and panic attacks easily qualify, but this seemed pretty on-the-fence, maybe even a little bit on the wrong side of the fence."

"Yeah, it's weird, but it just snuck over."

"Good to know," I said.

"So what are you planning to do with Mr. Dull at one in the morning?" she asked.

"I don't know. I said something to him about bowling and coffee so probably that."

"Good luck with that," she said and chuckled.

"Yeah, it's going to be even more awkward to turn down the next date after he drove all the way here in the middle of the night, but you never know – maybe this is all happening for a reason."

"I thought you weren't really attracted to this guy anyway," she said.

"Come on. I'm not that shallow. I've dated guys I wasn't phys-ically attracted to before. Plus, maybe I'll see a totally different side of this guy tonight, something that makes him look better than he did on those first two dates when his bland face seemed to just blend into the background."

"Good luck with that," she said. "I'm going to go back to sleep. Call me when he leaves."

"Will do."

*

As I waited for Himesh to arrive, it occurred to me that maybe I had given up on him too easily. There were crimes far worse than being dull. In fact, I had read once that boring men often make the best husbands. With nothing on TV and no one making noise in the parking lot, I watched the living room clock slowly tick from one minute to the next and tried to get excited for his arrival.

Just before 1:30, he was there. "Hey," he said with a smirk on his face. "Bet you didn't think I'd really show." It hadn't even occurred to me that he might not show up.

"Yeah, I wondered a little," I said.

"Should I put this in the bedroom?" he asked and held out a black backpack.

"What did you bring?"

"Just a few necessary items," he said with that same smirky expression. Maybe I had judged him too soon. He seemed more alive and less rigid than he had the other two times, and his face, with its understated features that could belong to anyone was somehow more defined. I remembered comparably common-faced people who, over time, became as distinct as anyone and realized my attraction-mechanism may have been discarding candidates too quickly. Before that moment, Himesh was as generic as the encyclopedia picture beside the caption *person of Indian descent*, but something about that smile made his mud-colored eyes and skin glow like the glossy wrapping-paper typically saved for a glamorous gift.

"You can just set it here. We're going out anyway," I said.

"We are?"

"Yeah. You didn't think we were going to sit here all night and watch movies, did you? I'm a better host than that."

He looked confused and said, "I suppose going out for a while might be fun. What were you thinking?"

"If you're hungry, there's IHOP. If not, bowling at the all night alley is usually interesting."

"I never eat after ten, so I guess bowling, but I didn't bring any socks," he said, looking down at his sandaled feet.

"No worries. The alley has a sock vending machine. It's all good."

"I really don't mind hanging out here," he said. "Want to give me a tour?"

"We can do that later. There's really not much to see."

*

I could tell he was getting restless after the first hour of bowling, but I had optimistically paid for two hours. If we were going to successfully complete an all-night date, the time had to be filled up somehow, and a hands-on activity like bowling helped to keep energy levels high and stave off the onset of exhaustion.

There were only two other patrons in the alley at that late hour, a very large middle-aged man with sunburned skin and facial lines that made even his resting expression appear like a scowl, and a thin man who may have been in his thirties but was forced to wear the familiar beaten-down-by-life body and face due to a steady series of stressful experiences. Saturn Bowl, Beaumont's all night alley, was one of two bowling alleys in town, and I never understood how it stayed open. Palace Bowl, the much nicer alley in the better part of town, was usually busy, employed attractive young men and women, housed a restaurant with a surprising variety of entrees, and managed to keep its Caribbean colored surfaces polished and clean. Contrarily, Saturn Bowl was never busy, provided prices and décor not seen since the seventies, and stood on a street often frequented by prostitutes and drug dealers. Even though the smoking ban had been in effect for over a year, the stale smell and haze of smoke hung in the air and saturated the hair and clothes of those who entered the all night alley.

"What time are we paid through?" Himesh asked and looked at his watch again.

"Until 3:30 ... something like that," I said and grabbed the ball for my second throw.

Just before throwing the ball in an attempt to pick up the spare, I heard a loud, barbaric yell, stopped a step short of my release, and searched for the source. Several lanes over, the obese man in the tightly-fitting clothes was unraveling quickly. "I fuckin' told you! She's at home with Willy!" he shouted. I looked over at my nervous date and finished the throw, a distracted effort that ended with my ball in the gutter.

As Himesh approached the ball return, things were escalating between the only other pair in the alley. I noticed the sole overnight employee watching the two men as he pretended to be busy spraying shoes with sanitizer. "Don't you talk like that no more! You keep saying that shit and I'll whoop you," the obese man screamed.

Himesh set his ball back on the ball return, walked over to my chair, and said, "I think we need to get out of here."

"Oh, it's fine. Just keep playing. They're not paying any attention to us."

"That's it!" the large man shouted to his soft-spoken friend and proceeded to violently pull off his own shirt, a gesture I didn't know how to decipher.

"Seriously, let's go," Himesh pleaded.

"I'm not walking past those guys right now. I think we're safer here," I said.

"Oh, my God. This is getting weird," Himesh said as the obese guy kicked off his shoes and pulled off his sweat pants. "Why is he doing that?"

"I don't know. How would I know?" I said. "Aren't you going to bowl?"

"Am I going to bowl? Are you serious? I'm not turning my back to this freak show."

The obese man lunged at his friend but failed to make contact.

"Stop it, Corey. Calm down," the friend said.

"You talk shit too fuckin' much, man, and I'm sick an' tired of it. Sunny and I are just fine."

"Dude, that ain't true. You gotta listen to me. I'm telling you – I saw her and that Carlos dude," the friend said. With that, the nearly-naked obese man grabbed a bowling ball off the nearest rack, walked toward the lane in typical bowler fashion, but didn't throw the ball toward the pins. Instead he turned back toward his friend, right before reaching the release line, and hurled the ball in his friend's direction. Of course the aim of a drunk, angry man throwing a fifteen pound ball was poor, so his friend was spared the intended results and was instantly as fired-up as the red-faced obese man in the white briefs. "Dude, what the fuck?" he shouted. "I tried to be your friend. I tried to help, but I'm done with this bullshit!"

"Do you want me to just take your turn?" I asked Himesh.

"How can you think about bowling right now? This is insane," he said.

"Come on. Play through the pain," I said.

"I really don't think that saying applies here. We're not in any pain. He is," he said and subtly nodded in the direction of the struggle between the two men. By this point, the obese man had tackled his friend to the floor and appeared to be aggressively pulling his shaggy hair.

"I'm pretty sure that saying doesn't specify who is in pain," I said.

"It's clearly implied."

"Whatever. Do you want to bowl or not?" I asked just before two police officers rushed into the alley, approached the two men, and quickly neutralized the situation. "See. All's well," I said and received an eye-roll from Himesh.

"All's well?" he shouted. "I'm glad you think so."

The alley employee approached us and said, "Sorry about that, folks."

"It's okay. It's not your fault," I said.

"Ain't that the truth? But, I must admit, scuffles like that keep me awake on these overnight shifts."

"It must be pretty stressful working here overnight," I said.

"Oh, it is, but that's kind of the reason I like it. I wouldn't be here if I didn't," he said and flashed me a nearly-toothless grin. "This kinda shit is what keeps me going, gets me out of bed. You see, I ain't got nothin' but this place, ain't got nothin' but the chance of seein' some shit go down. Everyone else is asleep, but I'm here. I'm here havin' adventure and stayin' out all night. You ain't never know who gonna walk through that door."

"I know what you mean," I said, half meaning it, and looked over at a disgusted looking Himesh.

*

An hour later, we were sitting at Bayou City Café, and Himesh's mood was deteriorating rapidly. "How long are we going to stay here?" he asked.

"Well, we still have two hours until sunrise, and there isn't much open right now, but wouldn't it be cool to watch the sun rise over Beaumont here at the coffee shop, to usher in the day with a warm beverage and a muffin?"

"No, not really."

"Well, what would you suggest? The only other open places are Walmart, the grocery store, IHOP, and a couple of gas stations along the highway."

"Let's just go back to your place," he said and slumped a little further into the armchair he occupied.

"There's really nothing to do there. I have Monopoly, but I think we're too tired for that."

"Right now I just want to go home," he said and took the last sip of his coffee.

"No. Come on. Just settle in a little and relax," I said.

"Like at the bowling alley? I've gotta say, I'm beginning to wonder what kind of girl you are to be so calm when those guys were fighting. It's kind of a turn-off, to be honest – a girl who is so fearless."

"Well, first of all, thanks for that honesty," I said sarcastically. "And, second of all, I was only calm because you were so nervous. That's typical of my temperament – of the temperament of a lot of people, it seems – to take on the reverse role of the person they're with as a way of balancing out the situation."

"So that's how you do things? You just do the opposite of the person you're with so that no one's happy?" he asked.

"It usually has better results than this," I said and watched a young Asian couple, drunk and affectionately wrapped in each other's arms, walk through the glass doors.

"Okay," he said.

"So I'm going to go way out on a limb here and say you're not having a good time," I said and flashed back for a moment to my disastrous Sadie Hawkins date of sophomore year in high school when I asked out a senior who had no interest in going with me and made his disinterest known by never looking directly at me and slow dancing with enough space between us to comfortably accommodate a third person. At the end of the dance, when I apologized to the guy for inviting him to a dance he didn't want to attend, he said, "That's okay. It's my fault for saying yes. I knew I wouldn't have a good time, but thanks for trying."

"You're pretty perceptive," Himesh said.

"Yeah, it was a little hard to tell, but luckily I took a couple of psychology classes in college."

"This is why I like to make plans. It never turns out well if I don't," he said.

"I usually make plans too. Trust me. You should see my calendar. It's full of plans," I said.

"Yeah, I bet."

"Seriously, it's full of plans and schedules," I said, leaning in a little with wide open eyes. "I'm a very organized person."

"Okay, I believe you," he said.

"I even have one of those calendars with the extra months so I can write stuff down way in advance."

"A sixteen month calendar?"

"Yeah," I said.

"You've got to be fucking kidding me!" Either this subject really hit a nerve or Himesh had just slammed hard into the wall of extreme exhaustion that held the power to provoke irrational behavior.

"What?"

"Sixteen month calendars are so fucking stupid. What's the point of purchasing a calendar with those extra months? It's not like people who buy sixteen month calendars can start at the seventeen month mark when they buy the new one. No. They just waste the money and paper for no reason. I mean, it would be a

different story if there was just a totally separate column of calendars that ran on that sixteen month schedule. You know, you
buy the first one that starts at, say, April and goes to July, and
then the next calendar picks up with August. Granted, it would be
a little ludicrous for the calendar industry to completely rewrite
the definition of a year for no apparent reason. But the point I'm
trying to make is that that's not how it works at all. You just have
four extra months there for no damn reason, so what the hell's the
point?"

Engaging in a real exchange seemed too risky given his current
state, so I just said, "Yeah, I guess I see what you're saying."

"And the only reason I can even think of as to why someone
would buy a sixteen month calendar is out of sheer laziness ...
for the kind of people who are too fucking lazy to buy a new
calendar on time and put off the purchase for months. I mean,
who are these people anyway?"

"Like I said, the extra months come before January," I chimed
in.

"You mean the calendar starts four months before the new
year, that they just repeat the last four months of the previous
year?"

"Yeah."

"Then what the hell is the point of that? Who would buy that?
What a waste!"

"Like I said, I like to write down my plans in advance."

"Then why not just write it down on the previous calendar
since you already paid for the pages? You're being totally irrational."

"I guess I never really thought about it," I said and took a sip
of my cocoa.

"And that's the problem with people today. They never think
about anything logically. You think it's a good idea to go bowling
in the middle of the night but don't register the possible problems
with that plan. You think it's okay to lure a guy over the state
border in the middle of the night with false pretenses and then

are shocked that he's upset."

"False pretenses?" I asked.

"Never mind. Can we please just go back to your place and get some rest? I'm exhausted."

"Okay."

*

Himesh fell asleep quickly, leaving me the opportunity to satisfy my instincts and snoop in his backpack. I unzipped the large pouch quietly, looked over to make sure he was sleeping, and opened up the bag. There, right on top of an orange towel, was a small box of condoms, the kind sold at gas stations and small drug stores. "Oh, my God," I said aloud.

Himesh grunted something unintelligible, jerked awake quickly, and looked over at me. "What the hell?" he said.

"You brought condoms?"

"You're going through my stuff?"

"You brought condoms?"

"Yeah. So what?" he said.

"Why?"

"What do you think?"

"You thought we were going to have sex?"

"Of course I thought we were going to have sex. It's our third date," he said.

"Third date? You mean that Hollywood crap about having sex on the third date? You actually believe that?"

"Why the hell else would I drive out here in the middle of the night?"

"Oh, my God. You thought our Facebook conversation was a booty call, that I asked you here for sex?"

"Yes!"

"Oh," I said. How had I not realized that? Why would I think this guy I didn't know would want to drive an hour at midnight just to spend time with me? "So you've actually had sex on a third date before?"

"Sure, sometimes the second ... sometimes the first."

"Well, I'm not going to have sex with you, but I do have three different kinds of ice cream."

"No thanks. I'll pass."

I dished up a bowl of mint chocolate chip ice cream with cherries, chocolate syrup, whipped cream, and a banana, a respectable attempt to salvage an otherwise unpleasant evening. The sunrise streamed through the thin curtain that covered my dining room window, and Himesh sat slouched over at my kitchen table.

"Are you the kind of person who could be happy just making someone else happy?" he asked as I sat down. I sensed he was fishing for something.

"Yeah, of course. I love the feeling of donating food to the food shelf, and sometimes, when I stay at a hotel, I give the maid a twenty and write a little thank you note on the complimentary notepad."

"Good because not watching you eat ice cream for breakfast would make me happy," he said, sitting there looking smug.

"Okay ... well, that's different. I like legitimately making other people happy, but I don't like doing what I'm told just because someone has a false sense of superiority."

"Oh, this is legitimate, and it has nothing to do with superiority. It's seriously making my stomach turn looking at all that sugar. Don't you worry about your weight?"

"Look," I said, took a huge chocolaty bite, and continued to talk while chewing, "My body is my body, and sometimes I like ice cream for breakfast. I love making people happy. I'm a good person, but trying to make someone else happy by not eating something I love ... well, that's different."

"How is it different?"

"Okay—you know that sound the package of Ho Hos makes just as you rip it open?" He looked confused. "Well, sometimes I live for that sound. If a student yells at me or I have a huge stack of papers that are taking forever to grade or I'm on the date from hell, I think about that sound and even the cool texture of the plastic casing."

"So just open the thing, hear the damn sound, and throw the poison away," he said.

"First of all, don't refer to chocolaty goodness as poison, and second of all, it's not the sound itself. It's what it represents."

"So you're no better than Pavlov's dog?" he said.

"I guess not, and I'm okay with that," I said and took another sugary bite of sundae.

"This is just gross."

"You don't have to watch me eat then. You're free to leave."

"Well, thanks for giving me permission to do what I was about to do anyway," he yelled.

"This is unbelievable."

"What?"

"You acting like you're actually mad that I'm eating a sundae. You just wanted to have sex with me, and you're blaming the ice cream for your sexual frustration."

"Here's a little advice – when a guy agrees to go out with a girl who he has nothing in common with and would never even consider marrying, he wants to get laid. Period!"

"Fine!" I shouted. "And here's a little advice for you – if a guy wants to *get laid* he doesn't use words like *get laid* to describe it, and he doesn't act like a critical ass around the girl he wants to sleep with."

He stood up, walked briskly to the bedroom to grab his bag, and returned to the dining room. "Do you really think people use online dating to find a relationship? Are you really that fucking stupid? I know you have some bullshit masters in the arts, but you should at least be able to figure that out. Everyone knows online dating is for hook-ups. Who the hell would want to marry someone they met online?" he shouted.

"Who the hell would want to marry you ... no matter where they met you?" I yelled as he shoved his feet back into the sandals that brought him to my apartment six hours earlier. "Have a nice drive back," I said sarcastically, and he slammed the door behind him.

I stood still for a moment and could almost feel another woman in a nearby apartment, someone I would never know, lying cozy in her bed with a smile on her face after listening to another short-lived romance explode in her ears. It felt good to give something back to the community. After all, I had lived at Rosemont Apartments for about three years and had been gifted far more dramatic conversations than I had given.

Chapter Eleven: Students

Teaching college in Beaumont, Texas, had its challenges. With a student population flooded with first-generation college students and students who graduated from the barely-accredited high schools in Beaumont and the crime-ridden inner-city schools of Houston, many of my English students struggled to keep up with their course work. The landscape of the university was beautiful with its lush rows of palm trees and its elegant fountains surrounded by orange and fuchsia flowers, but across the street from campus the smoke from the chemical plant filled the sky with constant gray puffs of pollutants. Within the perimeter of campus, police officers and security cameras kept the place safe, but beyond its borders stood run-down neighborhoods with intense poverty and some of the highest crime rates in the state.

It was the beginning of another late Tuesday afternoon American Literature class, and my students were settling into the orange desk chairs that had been there since the building's last remodel in the mid-seventies. I rolled the old lectern to the side of the room, preferring to hold the heavy course book myself, and announced, "Hey, guys. Go ahead and open your books to page 674." I scanned through the attendance sheet, searched the room to see who was missing, and placed a black dot by the names of the students who weren't there. I erased the word fragments left

167

on the chalkboard by the professor before me, that angry looking heavy-set man who rushed from room to room with a face that always looked flustered, and I accidentally wiped white chalk dust across the front of my black pants.

"So before we get into the details of the text, before we discuss Thoreau's opinions on fashion and postal service and social conventions, before we talk about the essay assignment, I just want to start with one idea," I said and picked up a piece of chalk. "So Thoreau spends a lot of time in Walden writing about how he wants to live a life that is free of commitments for as long as he can, how he doesn't like the idea of being tied down to any one thing," I said. I looked at the students, saw the way they stared at me, like they were waiting to hear something interesting or important, and wondered how many of them had bothered to read the assignment before coming to class. "Who can tell me one choice Thoreau makes that shows his desire to avoid commitment?"

"He doesn't work much, doesn't really appear to even have a job," Macy said.

"Good. What else?"

"He isn't married," Sharquella said.

"Good. What else?"

"He doesn't own much stuff, right?" Trey said.

"Yes, good. What else?"

"He seems to avoid other people," Dominique said.

"Yes, you're right, so why is all of this important to him? Why does he make these choices during the two years that the book takes place?" I asked.

"Maybe he's just lazy," Chris said. "Maybe he's like my cousin, Clarice. She don't do shit, just lays around smoking pot all day and watches those damn *Lifetime* movies, and she expects her mom to support her." I smiled and nodded, inwardly enjoying the way literature classes almost guaranteed tiny windows into the private lives of my students.

"Yes, a lot of people have criticized Thoreau this way, saying that his experimental way of living wasn't so much about challenging society's ideas as it was about him just not wanting to work, and it's hard not to see it this way when Thoreau himself writes about how wasteful it is to spend a life doing nothing but hard labor," I said.

"So he is lazy," Chris said. "Why we reading a book about some guy who don't care about anything, some guy who's just a free-loader?"

"But is he a free-loader?" I asked. "Is there any evidence in the text that he's not completely self-sufficient?"

"Yeah," Chris said. "It says he borrows stuff to build his house from friends." I smiled again, surprised and delighted that Chris had finally started reading the assignments.

"You're right. He does say that," I said.

"So he is," Chris said. "He's just lazy."

"But maybe it's more than that," said Sean, the student who always sat in the back row, the student who had never spoken in class before.

"Explain what you mean," I said and nodded at him.

"Well," he started. "I don't know. I'm not sure."

"Yes, you do. You started to disagree with the idea Chris presented. You started to say that maybe Thoreau isn't just lazy. Why don't you see this as laziness?" I asked and raised my eyebrows in an exaggerated way.

"I guess I just mean that maybe he's just trying to say ... at least this is how I'm looking at it ... that maybe he's saying a life can be a lot of things, that maybe success can be a lot of things, that what matters ... what really matters is how you define success, that you should live your life the way you believe is right and not just assume other people have the right answers for you."

"Yes," I half shouted. "You're absolutely right, and what you just said is basically the definition of transcendentalism, which is something we need to have at least a basic understanding of in order to really get to the core of Thoreau's ideas." I scribbled *transcendentalism* across the top of the chalkboard.

"And, if you think about it, writing a book is a ton of work, right?" Sean said. "I mean, most of us cringe at the idea of writing a three page essay, right? So the idea of sitting down and writing an entire book is proof that Thoreau's not totally lazy," he said and nodded at Chris.

"Yeah, you got me on that one," Chris said and laughed.

For the rest of class, I noticed the way Sean sat up a little taller in his seat, noticed how he leaned in to his book a little more, how he nodded along as other students answered my many questions. This was what I taught for, this possibility that at any moment someone's literary apathy could be momentarily shifted, the idea that I could convince even one student to care.

I thought about Thoreau, thought about how this man who died long before I was born chose to go live in the woods alone in search of his life's great adventure. I wondered what it must have been like for him those first weeks in the woods, wondered how many times he questioned his decision to live there, how many times he came close to giving up the experiment. I realized that maybe, in some small way, I was like Thoreau, spending years of my life in a place other people saw as undesirable.

To my students, Beaumont was boring. It was the kind of place you ended up if better opportunities never materialized, the kind of place you tried like hell to escape, the kind of place you had to give justifications for when asked where you're from. But for me, Beaumont was an adventure, a place I had to learn slowly, a place I needed to experience in order to stare straight into the fire of life, a place I was somehow starting to love.

Somewhere in the middle of class, it started to rain outside, a steady sideways downpour that soaked the stream of students walking by my classroom windows. But inside everything seemed full of light as we spent an hour discussing the things a man who died long ago had to say about life.

Chapter Twelve: Jude

Three months into being thirty, I had jury duty for the first time in my life, and it was also the first time I had stepped into the Jefferson County Courthouse since my divorce had been finalized three years earlier. As I looked around at the ramp leading up to the courtrooms and the high ceiling above the atrium, I realized I didn't remember any of it, and this lack of recognition surprised me. There were plenty of places I had only visited once that were deeply carved into the confines of my mind, like the small seaside café in Port Aransas where Blake and I sat on a white picnic table, watched seagulls swim in the surf, and ate crab cake sandwiches on an afternoon a few months before our wedding. I remembered that hour vividly, but I didn't remember this courthouse, and I knew why. I didn't want to remember it, didn't want to memorize that place where I shuffled in with eyes on the ground and hands in pockets and managed a spiritless "Yes" when the judge asked me if I intended to dissolve my marriage. That memory, like so many others from the last moments of my marriage, was so infrequently visited by my mind that it collected heavy coats of dust and sat hidden, like old tables in the corners of abandoned houses.

All the prospective jurors marched into a large room, found seats, and waited while the woman at the podium called names and gave assignments. My assignment was just thirty minutes later, so I followed my group of twenty other jurors out of the large room, up the ramp, and down the hall to the long benches outside of the courtroom. A middle-aged woman wearing a tight, leopard print top and faded black jeans sat beside me. "I hope this don't go all day," she said. "I sure hope this don't go all day, baby. I've got shit to do."

"Yeah, me too," I said.

The woman nervously pulled on the ends of her blonde-tipped short hair, took a tube of red lipstick out of her pink purse, and reapplied it somewhat haphazardly, not quite getting the upper lip line covered. She exhaled audibly and said, "I really hope I don't run into my ex here."

"Is he a lawyer?"

"Oh, God no. He's one of the cooks in the restaurant downstairs. They got good stuff in there ... if we're here all day. Course I can't eat there, but you could."

"Hopefully you won't see him then," I said and noticed a cute, long haired guy sit down on the other side of the woman.

We sat in silence for a moment, so I pulled a book out of my bag, but just as I opened up to my spot and put the bookmark back in my purse, the woman tugged on my sleeve. "Sorry to bother you, Ma'am. Sorry to bother you, but how would they know what kind of underwear we're wearing?"

"Huh?" I asked and closed the book.

"Why would it matter what kind of underwear we're wearing? I had no idea," she said frantically and nodded in the direction of a red sign that said *Do not enter courtroom without appropriate attire. No t-shirts, slippers, thongs, shorts, or tank tops.* I started to laugh, and she whispered, "I'm wearing a thong. What do I do? Tell that bailiff guy?"

I wanted to say yes but said, "No, no. That's not referring to underwear. That's what they used to call flips flops, you know, the shoes."

She half hugged me and said, "Oh, thank God. I thought I was going to have to go commando in there, and it's sometimes hard for me to concentrate without underwear on. You know what I mean?"

I didn't but nodded anyway. She got up to walk off some nervous energy, and the guy sitting beside her slid over and said, "Oh, good God. Some people are so stupid."

"I know, right?" I said. "And these are the people making important decisions in trials."

"Our justice system at its finest."

"Yeah, pretty much," I said, shaking my head.

"I'm Jude, by the way," he said and held out his hand.

"Hi. I'm Paige," I said a little too loudly as my entire body appeared to be undergoing a power surge from the electricity his warm handshake sent through me.

"Ever done this before?" he asked.

"No, have you?"

"Yeah. It's crazy. I'm twenty-six, and this is my third time doing jury duty. The other two times were a total wash. They just called us in to the courtroom to tell us we were dismissed, that the case had settled or something. That's probably what you can expect to happen today too."

"I hope so," I said and watched as he tucked loose hairs behind his ear. The dark, shoulder length hair and the old button-down shirt he wore and the way he squinted when he spoke all clarified the feelings Sam had tried to convey to me when he talked about how he wanted to leave Cassie but couldn't.

"And if this thing does go through, you can sure as shit bet that woman won't get picked ... and probably not that guy over there either," he said, nudged my side and tilted his head in the direction of a youngish black man who had cat-called *hey baby* to every woman between the ages of twenty and fifty who walked past him.

I nodded.

"Seriously, these lawyer people can smell stupidity."

"Yeah, my friend back home is a lawyer, and I think that's true," I said.

"And where's back home for you?"

"Minnesota."

"Nice. Nice. Maryland for me," he said, and there we were, two northerners sitting in a southern courthouse.

"Baltimore?"

"Yep. Moved here in high school, and good God was that some culture shock," he said, palmed his forehead, and shook his head.

"I know what you mean."

Thong-woman walked back over, looked at me confusedly, and said, "Wasn't I sitting there before?"

"Yeah, you were," Jude broke in. "When you left, I slid over."

"You slid over? Wasn't you here before too?"

"Yeah, I was here," he said and patted the empty bench space beside him. "And then I slid over to here."

She just stood there staring at the empty bench spot and then walked away again.

"What was that?" I asked Jude.

"Like I said, she's not going to be on the jury, so that hurts our chances of being dismissed if there is an actual trial. It's all so typical, isn't it? This idea of rewarding people for their stupidity really permeates our culture in this country, doesn't it? But hey, who knows ... this thing might not even get off the ground. What do you say ... if this thing wraps up early, you wanna grab lunch somewhere?"

"Sure," I said, maybe a little too enthusiastically for such a casual offer, and suddenly I was hoping, harder than the lawyers were, for a settlement.

*

"I met this guy today at jury duty. It was crazy. We just started talking, bonded over a mutual disrespect for stupid people, and then we ended up going to lunch together and talking all afternoon. We only left the restaurant because the waiter was obviously annoyed that we were still there and just drinking refills. His name is Jude. It was seriously the craziest day. I really like him," I spouted to Abby that night. "I think we're going out again tomorrow. It's so crazy that I could wake up this morning annoyed about having to go sit at jury duty and then this could happen."

"I don't like him," she said flatly.

"What? I haven't even told you anything yet. He's from Baltimore, huge baseball fan."

"I just get a bad feeling."

"What? From what?"

"His name is Jude," she said.

"Oh, God!" I shouted into the phone, likely loud enough for my neighbors to hear. "The stupid name thing again? It's a freakin' name! His parents probably picked it out of a baby book or something."

"I'm just saying ... don't act like you weren't warned. I should've known better myself when I met Judd. I knew this guy in high school named Judd, and he was kind of an asshole."

"This theory of yours is so stupid," I said. "A person does not pick their name ... just like a person doesn't pick where they're born."

"No, but where they are born affects the way they are. Come on, do you really think you would be the same person if you were born in India or Ethiopia?"

"Maybe not. Okay, so that was a bad example, but a name is just a name. It's just a few letters that make a sound that indicates a certain person is a certain person. I would be the same if my name were Connie or Paige or Samantha."

"I disagree," she said.

"So you shouldn't have dated Judd because some guy in high school was a jerk? Then what if some girl in high school named Paige was mean to you? Does that mean we wouldn't be friends, that you would've avoided me when we met in college?" I asked.

"That never happened."

"I know. That's my point. What if it did?"

"It didn't, and you're ignoring the whole point of the theory."

"Which is what?"

"It doesn't matter that people don't choose their names. Their parents do. Name selection is not random. Why do you think people with fucked up names have fucked up lives?"

"Probably because of people like you."

"No, it's because they were raised by people stupid enough to pick the name, and if you're raised by a fool, chances are you'll be a fool."

"But Jude, or Judd, is not a fucked up name."

"It doesn't matter. The kind of person who picks that name is apparently the kind of person who raises that person in such a way that he turns into an asshole."

"You don't think there might be a little coincidence working here, that maybe you don't have a large enough sample size to really prove this theory?" I asked.

"Nope."

"Okay, but besides all of that. This guy's name is not Judd. It's Jude."

"Close enough," she said and sighed into the phone.

"Okay, well, that being said, he's very intelligent and attractive. He has this long, dark hair that keeps falling in his eyes when he talks. It's beyond adorable."

"Oh, no – the long hair thing? You just like those guys because of Matt," she said.

"No, I think it goes back further than that."

"There was someone before Matt? I thought he was your first boyfriend."

"He was, but I think it might be the Jesus thing."

"The Jesus thing?"

"Yeah, think about it. If you grow up in a church, you see this image of this guy who is supposedly the greatest man there ever was. It's all very attractive."

"So you want to have sex with Jesus?" she asked with an annoyed tone.

"No, not when I was in third grade ... or whenever it started, but there is something deeply ingrained there, some reason I was so drawn to Matt and his long hair in the first place."

"I don't get it. I grew up going to church too, and those long-hair guys always looked kind of greasy to me, like they always need a shower."

"Anyway, the point is that I'm really excited about this guy, and I haven't felt this way for a long time. I honestly haven't felt this since Blake and I started dating. I had to drive around for a half hour after the date just to scream in my car and release some of that excited energy," I said.

"So you feel the same way you felt with Blake at the beginning?"

"Yeah."

"Run."

"Abby, come on. I wasn't saying he is Blake. I was just saying my feelings are the same. I'm happy. Why can't you just be happy for me?"

"I'm worried. I can hear it in your voice. You're all excited, and your tone of voice is exhausting me."

"Because you're not happy?" I asked.

"No, because this much excitement at the very beginning of something isn't good. It never ends well."

"I don't think that's true," I said.

"We'll see."

*

After my conversation with Abby, I used the surplus of energy I was experiencing to clean my apartment. I worked through the mound of dishes, scrubbed bathroom floors, vacuumed the living room and both bedrooms, threw away the expired items in my fridge, and even individually dusted the small slats of my mini-blinds. When I had finished it all, I still wasn't tired. It was almost eleven, but my first class the next day didn't start until noon, so I decided to venture out and get a cup of cocoa at Bayou City Café.

The *café* was still relatively busy when I arrived. I grabbed my drink and found a table in the front room where I could grade quizzes while listening to the conversations around me and also survey the action in the parking lot.

After a few minutes and a few completed quizzes, the sound of a voice several tables away stopped me. It could have been Blake's in the way it sunk into all the room's crevices with that recognizable deepness, and suddenly I was sinking too, tunneling faster than I could dig myself out, falling back into the old expectations of where we would be if it had all been different. I sat still in my chair but felt myself pulled in the direction of that voice, completely disbelieving that the source could be the source – a short, gray wrinkled man – nothing like the young or future Blake. As the voice spoke about grandchildren and weather, I closed my eyes for a minute and walked my mind across the room to feel it all again, to be momentarily married to Blake one more time, at home right there in a little coffee shop in Beaumont, Texas.

*

The following night, Jude came over to my apartment. Under normal circumstances, I wouldn't have agreed to a man I had just met coming over so soon, but when he texted me earlier that day and said he was craving a pizza and a low-key evening, I couldn't help myself. I convinced myself that having a long lunch with someone was essentially the same as knowing a guy for several weeks, that I knew all I needed to know about him in order to grant him access to my home. The fact that my apartment was also immaculately clean served as the final argument and persuaded me to text him back with my address and an invitation.

Jude showed up twenty minutes late, but I didn't fault him for not possessing my Scandinavian compulsion for promptness, and when I opened the door to the sight of him holding the pizza palm-up like a French waiter and he said, "Delivery," I wanted to kiss him right then.

I offered him a beer from the twenty-four pack I had optimistically purchased that afternoon with the foolish assumption that he would be in my life long enough to finish them all. He loaded his plate up with pizza, but I just took one piece, knowing it would be a chore to even get through that with so much nervous excitement brewing inside me.

"I like your place. It's good we did this here," he said as he sat down on the sofa. "My place is pretty insane with four roommates and five dogs."

"Really? Wow."

"Yeah, I like my job at the liquor store. It's cool getting to meet so many interesting characters and all, but it doesn't exactly afford me a lavish lifestyle."

"That's overrated anyway," I said, and watched the artistic way he twirled the strings of excess cheese around the tip of the first slice with his fork before biting into it.

"It'd be nice to have some extra cash, though, you know, for traveling and stuff. There's a whole world beyond Beaumont and Baltimore, and I'd like to get out there and see it all." I nodded. "But I've got a plan. It's looking like Hardin County might finally lose their dry status at this next election. My roommate's got the dough, and I've got the know-how, so we're talking about opening up a liquor store in Lumberton right after it happens. Things are changing there. Young people are moving in, and it's about time those towns moved on. The prohibition can't last forever."

"True," I said and smiled.

I took tiny bites of pizza while he cruised through three pieces. I pretended to be consumed by the act of eating and sipping soda because I didn't know what to say, and he seemed content to sit and eat in the stifling silence. I told myself that it wasn't a big deal that we weren't talking, that he was just enjoying the pizza, but I had doubts and couldn't get comfortable. I noticed I was sitting with perfect posture like someone at a job interview, and I held the soda can with my pinkie out like a child pretending to drink tea. I felt strangely out of place in my own apartment.

"Mind if I get another beer?" Jude asked, breaking the silence.

"Wow, you finished that first one fast."

"Oh, I'm not done yet. It's just nice to have another one on hand. I just love that feeling of going straight from one bottle to another, makes me feel like I'm at a restaurant with awesome service, you know, the kind of place that's completely in tune with my needs. Don't misinterpret what I'm saying, though," he said and stood up. "I'm no alcoholic. I usually just have two or three, but it's nice to have that feeling of no lag time between sips, even though I'm my own waiter." He grabbed two beers, came out into the living room, put his hand over the light switch and said, "Mind if I flip this off?" He smiled, flicked the switch on and off a couple of times and said, "Artificial lightning is fun, but darkness ... darkness is better."

"Yeah, sure, you can turn it off if you want, but are you sure you want to finish your pizza in the dark?" I asked, wondering if maybe he had an acute sensitivity to light like my mom did or if he was preparing to make a pass at me.

"I'll open these drapes here. Then we'll have a little light – not that pepperoni and cheese on a slab of dough need to be viewed to be enjoyed. Presentation is not really key here," he said and pulled open the patio drapes to let the lights from the parking lot blanket the living room with dim ambiance. He grabbed the beers off the counter and came back to the couch, but this time he sat on the floor and used the couch for a backrest. "Isn't this better?" he asked, holding his arms out to the atmosphere of darkness. "I like to be comfortable."

"Yeah, it's good."

"It is indeed. It always seems like people are more of themselves in the dark, like when the light is stripped away they can really talk to each other."

Just then we heard a car door slam outside and a woman yell, "What the hell am I supposed to do with this? This ain't even close to my size. Do I look like a stick woman to you?"

"I thought you said you was a fourteen," her female companion yelled back. "That's why I told Ronnie to make yours the same size as Maida's."

"A fourteen? A fourteen? Can you see me? Are you freakin'

kiddin' me? Do I look like a fourteen? I ain't been a fourteen since middle school. I ain't no fourteen!" she said, emphasizing the word fourteen like it was something to be ashamed of.

"Well, maybe this'll be some motivation – make you lose a little 'fore the weddin'."

"Oh, hell no! Hell no! Ronnie just gonna have to make me notha one. I ain't losing nothin'!"

"Wow, these walls don't keep anything out," Jude said. "It must be kind of annoying."

"No, actually it's not. Actually, I kind of love it. It's kind of comforting to be connected by sound to all these people ... makes me feel less alone up here," I said, surprising myself by saying it, by so freely admitting to my loneliness, but something about hearing those women shouting outside pulled me out of my shy state.

"I can see that. I guess loneliness is never really a factor for me living in the crazy house. An average night there consists of at least eight people, sometimes more. I don't need noise from strangers when I have sex sounds and dogs barking and TVs blaring and guitars turned way up right in my own house."

"That actually sounds pretty great."

"Yeah, you'll definitely see it sometime."

"Cool," I said, feeling awkward sitting so much higher than he was. I walked my plate back to the kitchen, grabbed another cherry coke, and sat down on the floor beside him when I got back.

"And my friends will be pretty surprised when they meet you."

"Why's that? Don't you date much?"

"Oh, ha! No, that's not it. You're just not the typical girl I go for. It's always blondes and more the actress kind of body type, but I like you. I had a lot of fun the other day after our jury duty dismissal."

"Yeah, me too."

"And it's likely I'm not your ideal physical specimen either," he said with a playful tone of voice that somewhat betrayed the insincerity of the statement.

"Well ... that's not true."

"Well, anyway it's time for me to try something new. Those girls always end up complaining that I'm just a liquor store employee. They always want to know when I'm going to magically turn into a lawyer or teacher or something. Like this last girl I dated, Holly, she said she was cool with my job, but then we hit the six month mark – it always seems to happen around then – and suddenly there was all this pressure to go back to school or apply for management positions. She even brought me an application from the bank her dad works at – like I'm the kind of guy who works at a bank. She was totally fine with what I do at first, back when I was bringing twelve packs to her parties, but then it all changed, and she was suddenly ashamed of me. It always happens that way."

"That's horrible."

"Yeah."

"I say that a job is a job. As long as you can pay your bills, it's all good."

"And the whole hierarchy of positions in this country is so ridiculous. Why is it so impressive that someone practices law or medicine? Why do those careers get their own language to describe them? Why can't I say I practice liquor distribution? Isn't that just as much of a part of our society as fixing a sprained elbow?" I chuckled, and he went on. "And what is this obsession the last three women I've dated have with me becoming a teacher ... and not just any kind of teacher ... an elementary school teacher. Who even remembers their first grade teacher? I don't, but you can sure as shit bet a whole lot of people remember me now. I'm the one standing there when they walk into the utopia of their desires."

"I don't drink much, but I like your point. A liquor store *is* an integral part of our society. I'm a teacher, and I love what I do and see a tremendous amount of value in it all, but I don't hold my job over any other, and in a way, learning and liquor have always existed together, right?" I paused and looked at my coke, then continued. "I mean, think about it – look at any small town in America. What do you usually see? A little school, a bar or two, and a liquor store ... more liquor than learning, in fact. I guess most people need a little alcohol in this life. Look at Lumberton. Yes, it's a dry city, but that just means people drive down to Beaumont to get what they need. They're not doing without."

"Exactly."

"If your job wasn't important to them, why would they make such an effort to get to you?"

"They know it's important, but they're ashamed of that, and as a result of their shame, my job is deemed low – low paying and low class."

"I never thought about it that way, but you're right," I said.

"So you don't drink?"

"A little, but no, not really, not much anyway. It's not a moral thing for me. I just don't really like the taste, and I hate feeling out of control. I'm kind of a control freak and don't like to put myself in unpredictable situations."

"And yet you invited me over here after only knowing me a couple of days?"

"Yeah, I guess you just seemed okay. You didn't seem like the guy my friend, Sara, met online."

"That sounds like a story."

"Oh, it is."

"Well ..."

"Okay, so my friend was doing the online dating thing—"

"Huge mistake," he said, and I nodded instead of admitting I too had ventured into the world of online men.

"Yeah, so she met this guy online who lived in a small town in Western Louisiana, maybe an hour from here or so. They emailed back and forth for a few weeks, and he seemed like a nice guy and all, so they made plans to get together. She travels sometimes for her job and was going to be in his area, so she agreed to have dinner with him at a restaurant near his house."

"Okay—"

"And here comes the interesting part of the story. So she made one major dating mistake."

"She went to his place to pick him up?"

"Exactly."

"It's a classic scenario really."

"Yeah, and because they had been emailing she was convinced he was something that he wasn't. Okay ... so she agreed to meet at his place before dinner so they could ride together. She drives out to this run-down house in the middle of swamp country Louisiana, drives down a long gravel driveway to get to this house that is hidden from the rest of society. You know, the whole bit. She gets to the house; he invites her in for a minute and asks her if she'd like a drink. There are two glasses of wine already poured, so she declines, and God knows what was in those drinks. And here comes the creepy part. She notices that there is a flickering coming from a room down the hall and asks the guy what that's about."

"Candles? He thought he was going to get laid right off, before dinner?"

"Yes, candles, but weirder. He tells her he got a hot bath ready, that he thought she might want to shave her legs before dinner."

"Didn't see that coming!"

"I know, and the more you think about it, the creepier it gets. She just grabbed her purse and ran out of there ... didn't give the guy an explanation. He emailed a few times after that, trying to set up another try, but she just ignored the emails and shut down her online dating account shortly after the bath incident."

"I don't blame her. Either the guy wanted to kill her, or he doesn't understand the standard progression of dating," he said.

"Doesn't understand? Come on; there is no way a guy would think that's normal."

"Seriously, think about it. Think about movies, about the way they portray things. Take *The Bridges of Madison County*, for example."

"You've seen *The Bridges of Madison County*?"

"Yeah, it was my ex's favorite movie."

"Okay."

"Think about it, though. Those people knew each other, what, like two days, and they were in the bath together."

"But my friend had just met this guy."

"But not really, though. They had been writing, and sometimes writing can be more intimate than talking in person. Hell, why do you think sexual relationships progress so much further in the texting age than they did before? People will say things in writing that they would never normally say," he said and looked at me with a prideful smirk on his face.

"Damn. Only you would be able to present an argument that could actually get the creepy bath guy off the hook a little ... but I still think he was planning to rape her."

"Yeah, probably, but you never know. Sometimes people, and situations, are more complicated than you think."

"Yeah, sometimes ..."

"Do I spot a CD tower?" he asked, leaning his body around the coffee table to see beyond the far end of my green, wrap-around couch.

"You do."

"This should be very telling," he said and crawled over to the tower in the shadowed corner of my living room. "Cranberries – nice!"

"I haven't listened to them since high school," I said, turned the lamp on, and joined him back on the floor.

"Radiohead, Coldplay, Morphine, and good God, you must like Tori Amos. Hey, did you know you have two copies of this one?"

"Yeah, I wore out the first one in college, so I had to buy a new one."

"And you saved the old one? Why?"

"I don't really know. I'm not a packrat person at all, but I just couldn't throw it out. *Little Earthquakes* was my favorite album for a really long time, and tossing it in the trash – even though it skips like crazy and doesn't play anything past track six – just felt wrong."

"I can respect that," he said. "But I can't respect this." I started to laugh. "Mariah Carey? Mariah ... fucking ... Carey?"

"It was my ex husband's," I said. "He didn't take everything with him when he moved out."

"Please tell me he's also responsible for the *Titanic* sound-track."

"He is," I lied.

"Phew," he said and made the hand-swipe-across-the-forehead motion. "I've never heard of Kory and the Fireflies."

"Oh, yeah, they're kind of a local band ... well, not local as in here, local in South Dakota. They're good but not as good as Space Rocket Jones," I said, holding up the robot-clad case. "Space Rocket has a similar sound, but their singer's more unique, and the drummer's phenomenal."

"You know, I've never seen a firefly. I've seen rockets but never a firefly," he said, suddenly serious with sad eyes staring at the stack of CDs.

"Really?" I asked but wondered if he might be lying.

"Yeah, it was one of the great disappointments of my child-hood – right up there with the Orioles losing to the Yankees in the playoff game of ninety-six."

"Really?"

"Yeah, we were the wild card that year and—"

"No," I interrupted him. "I mean the firefly thing. I'm sur-prised you've never seen them, and that it was such a big deal."

"Oh, yeah, it was like anything else in my childhood, some-thing my brother used to torment me. He used to come running inside, claiming there were fireflies in the yard, but by the time I got my shoes on, and rushed out there, they were always gone. After a while, I stopped putting my shoes on altogether, which once led to stepping on ... what I still think was a strategically placed ... nail."

"Really? That's awful."

"It's just a brother thing."

"I have a brother, and he never left nails in the yard for me to step on."

"It's different with guys. Besides, I don't think he ever really forgave me for being born. I guess I stole his thunder, so to speak."

"So he pretended to steal your lightning," I said, proud of my pun.

"Yeah, except it wasn't so much about stealing as it was about having – having something I didn't have, seeing something I had never seen. Sometimes I just sat out there in the back of the yard, waiting for them to come, but they never did, not for me."

"I bet they were never really there," I said.

"I don't know. To this day, he claims they were, and he's almost thirty now. Then again, he was almost sixteen the last time he called me outside. It had been several years since the last time, and I hadn't thought about fireflies much, but I still wanted to see them, so I went out. To this day, he claims that was the only time he made it up, the only time it was all for a prank."

"What happened?"

"I ran out there, my brother pointed me in the right direction, and I saw the blinking for the first time, coming from some bushes in the side yard. I kneeled down, reached my hand out to try to catch it, and my brother's stupid friend, Marcus Willbaster, jumped out of the bushes and grabbed me." I started to laugh. "He had been lying in there, flicking the switch of one of those tiny lights you win in video arcades. I had always hated that guy, and the firefly incident only intensified those feelings."

"I can imagine."

"I guess I've always kind of chased after beautiful things," he said. "It's why I fell so hard for Holly. It was nothing else, just the way she looked. How stupid is that?" I didn't respond. "And hell, that's probably why she chose me too, and don't get me wrong, it was pretty great for a while. It was pretty fucking great," he said and took a swig of beer. "But then, after the sex rush had been pretty much played out, there we were, just two people sitting in a room together. I dated her for almost a year, and we never even talked to each other. I mean, sure, we talked, but not really about anything. I never even told her the firefly story, and I've known you a week," he said and looked at me.

"I know what you mean, but the thing is ... if you're not attracted to me—"

"Oh – no, that's not what I meant. I think you're cute," he said. "I definitely think you're cute," he said again, maybe trying to convince himself more than me.

"Okay."

"I just like that I can talk to you without being so ... distracted."

"You know, you might be right. I think I chose my ex-husband based on his looks ... and his voice. He had this voice that I can't really describe except to say it had music in it, like a bright trumpet sound but with a deep quality," I said, sighed, and leaned against the cold wall. "It's hard to describe, but hearing him speak was like the first time I heard music. Even when we were just friends, long before we ever dated, I knew my life would never be the same, and it wasn't."

"Yeah," Jude said and flipped off the light above us. "I think I know what you mean." I knew he was talking about Holly, but when he looked at me with those dark eyes framed by the shadows of the room and leaned in for a kiss, it didn't matter.

*

We stayed up late that night talking, kissing, drinking sodas and beer, playing video games, talking and kissing again, and eventually we ended up in my bed, but only for the comfort of pillows and more conversation. Around four, Jude drifted off to sleep, but I was wide awake, too keyed up to even consider sleep.

I already knew it would end soon, that that night of bonding at my apartment would be the only one for Jude and me, but still it felt good having a beautiful man in my bed, lying there beside him and listening to him breathe peacefully for a while before heading out to watch a movie alone in the living room.

But I didn't turn on the TV. Instead I just sat there, replaying the events of the evening in my mind. I knew I wanted Jude, but, more than that, I wanted a man who found my voice and skin more calming than the slow seduction of sleep, a man who would pull me close and hum familiar melodies until my eyelids were heavy and sunk down like Spanish moss on trees, a man who would paint pictures on my skin until my limbs were loose like well-traveled walkways, and a man who would silence the sun's screaming demands to rise by staying in bed with me all morning.

That night I sat by the window and watched lovers kiss in the alley below and felt happy for no reason at all. Maybe it was the flicker of hope that Jude would love me. Maybe it was the lack of sleep and the caffeine rush working within me, or maybe it was the pleasure of watching those strangers kiss and knowing that someday I too would stand in the presence of one who knows.

※

It was hard to concentrate on my life. After meeting Jude, previously easy tasks felt tedious and unimportant. I struggled through grading essays, stopping frequently and starting over when my mind meandered away from the sentences on the page and over to Jude's hands on my skin. But in classes, my lectures soared. Everything being heightened meant my mind was too, and I almost danced across beige tiles as I taught sophomores about transcendentalism and free verse poetry.

One of the great things about teaching on a college campus was that so many pivotal life moments happened there, and sometimes that spring semester, I ventured out of my little office to sit outside and watch them happen.

March in Beaumont often delivered temperatures above eighty, and it felt freeing to be out in it while my friends in Minnesota endured their last flashes of winter. Students passed by in summer clothes, and rap music played on the speakers in front of the student center. One day, I tried to get some reading done but caught myself only half-reading the story I had assigned to my students, so I kept going back to the same three paragraphs to try to take my mind away from the surroundings and place it back in the book. Just when I was starting to really read what I was reading, a young woman rushed over to her friend sitting on the bench across from me. "Oh, my God, Meg! Oh, my God!" She was crying hysterically, tears streaming down her face and soaking her grey t-shirt. "I don't think I can do this. I know I can't do this," she screamed.

Her friend fumbled frantically through her purse and pulled out a tissue while I pretended to read but held the book unnaturally high to be able to look over it and onto the scene. "What's going on?" Meg asked.

"I really thought I could do this. God, I've been planning on doing this my ... whole ... life," she managed through sobs. "But I can't. I can't do it. It was awful."

"Slow down. What happened? Can you tell me what happened?" Meg asked.

Her whole body heaved with sobs before she started to explain. "We had to do the cadaver today ... dissect it. They said this would be hard, that this would be a huge challenge, that some people wouldn't go forward from there ... but I didn't think it would be ... me." She audibly inhaled and exhaled before going on. "I guess I never really thought about this ... didn't think it through ... didn't think about what it would really be like ... to do this. I was standing there, and he was dead, and I started thinking about it, really thinking about it," she said and started crying again. "I can't do this. I'm going to have to change my major. I can't go back there and finish the assignment. I can't. I ran out of there, had to get out of there."

"It's going to be okay," Meg said and put her arm around her. "You'll figure out something else to do."

"But this is what I always wanted, the only thing I ever saw myself doing ... and then, there he was ... dead. Dead. It's too much, and I never really thought about it ... about the death part of it. I just thought about the life part, the good part, but I can't do this," she said.

"You'll find something else to do," her friend said. "Come on, let's go get a coffee or something." They stood up to continue the conversation beyond my audible range.

I watched them walk toward the student center and wondered what life altering moments were unfolding in my own students' lives, and then I heard a clanging in my purse, the text message alert, and I was back in my own personal life again. I pulled the phone out and read the message from Jude: *I was wondering if a cute teacher I know would like to join me for dinner in Galveston on Saturday.*

I texted back: *Of course!*

Walking back to my office, I wondered if I had been wrong in my assessment of Jude's feelings. After all, Galveston Island was almost two hours away, a pretty elaborate third date for a guy who wasn't that interested in a woman.

Everything on the way back to my office looked different than before. The squirrels scrounging for food in red trash cans, the puddles that stretched over sidewalks from the downpour that morning, the groups of students smoking by buildings, and the silver storm clouds rushing in overhead all possessed a kind of mystical glow. My perspective had fully shifted, and it was too late to see things clearly.

*

The following night Sam joined me for a walk at Wuthering Heights Park. I had extra energy to dispose of, and he was dealing with yet another Cassie dilemma. Waiting in my car for Sam's truck to pull up, I saw a man exchange a handshake for a paper bag under the leaf-canopy of a large tree. The man with the bag walked off, but the other man walked straight toward my car. I kept waiting for him to change direction, but he kept walking toward me, so I started the car up again, pulled out of the lot, and drove around on side streets for a while. When I got back to the park, the men were gone, and Sam was there.

"Hey," I said, jumping out of the car.

"I'm kind of surprised I beat you this time. You're always early."

"Well, I actually—" I started.

"But anyway," he interrupted. "I have so much crap to tell you. You would not believe this week."

I nodded, said, "I believe it," and retied my tennis shoes.

"Why does she have to be so pretty? I am killing myself over this girl, and she is so nonchalant about everything, and why does she have to be so pretty?"

"Maybe you could just pretend she isn't."

"Not likely, and she makes me feel like I'm lucky just to be standing in her presence, like I should put up with anything she throws in my direction just so she won't leave the room."

"Well—"

"I know. I know. It's my own fault. I know. We've been over that, but I'm stuck, and I know she's been seeing Rick again ... or maybe someone else, but it doesn't matter who it is. I know it's happening. She keeps taking calls in the bathroom, like I'm an idiot ... says she's talking to her mom, like I'm an idiot."

"Well—"

"I know. I'm an idiot, but you should see her legs in these new shorts she always wears. She's torturing me ... those legs ... even when she hasn't shaved in a week ... it doesn't matter. What am I going to do? Even if I got away, ended it, even hearing her name, even part of her name ... hell, someone could say cass, just cass, and I would be back in it again. I would rush over to her house, and the whole thing would start from scratch."

"Luckily for you, cass isn't a real word."

"You know what I mean," he said, popped a piece of gum, and shoved the wrapper into his back pocket.

"I do know what you mean, and I'm a little worried myself."

"Don't worry. I'll figure it all out, eventually."

"No, I meant about myself, my own life."

"Oh, I thought you said things with that Jude guy weren't going to get off the ground."

"Yeah, that's what I thought, but then he asked me on a date, to Galveston."

"Galveston? Really? Like an overnight thing?"

"No, I don't think so. He asked me to have dinner with him there. What does that mean?"

"Don't be so paranoid. The guy likes you. He's trying to impress you with a really cool date. It's all pretty obvious."

"Maybe, but I don't know. He kissed me the other night, but it all felt very one-way, you know, like when you're young and spray some of your dad's cologne on a pillow, and you kiss the pillow and think about the guy you want, and you're thinking about it all so much that you actually feel things. It kinda felt like that." Sam gave me a strange look. "Shut up. At least I'm not wasting two years of my life with a girl just because she has pretty legs."

"I'll give you that."

"The thing is – nobody wants to settle. We all want to feel like we've really captured something. The very idea of settling is a terrifying thought, but isn't it even more terrifying to be the one settled upon?" I asked.

*

By the time Jude drove his red hatchback onto the ferry, the sun was already starting to set and stood straight ahead out over the darkening water. "Do you want to get out of the car and look at the scenery or stay in here?" he asked.

"Get out ... I think ... Yeah, definitely get out."

We made our way up the stairs and over to the lookout point at the front of the ferry. I stood there clutching the railing as the ferry pushed off and away from the shore. My wild red hair waved in the wind, and I felt beautiful in my new black sunglasses, pink painted toes peeking out from tan sandals, and a little black t-shirt over khaki shorts. I looked over at Jude, but it was clear he wasn't looking at me; he was looking at a perky little blonde in tight shorts and a tiny bikini top. I watched the waves smash against the sides of the ferry and saw two dolphins leap out of the distant waters, and I understood there was nothing I could do. Jude pointed up to a seagull hovering directly above us and put his arm around me, but it didn't matter. He kept looking over at the blonde, and I knew I couldn't compete with a girl like that.

After the bikini blonde made her way back downstairs and away from view, I affectionately rubbed Jude's arm that he was resting on the railing, but he didn't look at me. He stared straight out at the sun slowly sinking through the depths of a hazy horizon. I tasted the salt of the sea sky on my lips and realized that evenings so perfect would exist with future lovers, that Jude's peripheral vision blurred his ability to see me but that someday a man would stare harder at the contours of my body than at the outstretched landscape surrounding me.

As we pulled up to the island and the ferry settled into the terminal, Jude spoke enthusiastically about the shrimp fajitas that awaited us, but I wanted to be back home. I was afraid he would notice my miserable mood, and just as we pulled up to the restaurant, he did. "What's up with you? You haven't said much since we got off the ferry."

"Nothing. I think I'm just hungry," I said.

"Are you sure?" he asked. I nodded. "Come on. Pretend you're on trial. Would that be your answer?" I nodded again. "Because part of the problem with my relationships has always been the sea of bullshit we're constantly wading through. Seriously, if I did something, I want to know."

"Okay," I said, paused a moment, and went on, "The thing is

– I saw you ... noticed you notice that blonde girl on the ferry."

He paused for a moment and furrowed his brow, pretending to search for the subject I brought up, and then said, "Oh, yeah, well, that's because ... that's because that girl looked a hell of a lot like my cousin, Carrie. I kept looking at her because Carrie and I haven't seen each other in a couple of years, and I was trying to make sure it wasn't her."

"Really?"

"Really. I promise."

"Okay, good." Maybe he wasn't lying, I told myself. Maybe the girl on the ferry really did look like this Carrie cousin. Maybe he would show me a picture of this Carrie on Facebook later, and we'd both have a good laugh about the whole thing. I knew better, of course, but the possibility kept the evening alive.

*

Back at my apartment that night, I had completely forgotten about the ferry ride into Galveston. The shrimp dinner at Pelican Paradise Cove and the moonlight beach walk after dinner had erased the memory of the blonde, just like the night waves washed away footprints of the sand's daylight visitors.

Jude shook the sand out of his shorts and into my bathtub and said, "I'll never understand the sand thing. How does it get everywhere?"

"I know, right? I'm pretty sure I have sand in my bra, and we didn't even go in the water."

"I guess it's just in the air," he said and treated me to a playful smile. "Maybe we should check you for sand."

"It sounds like you're talking about wood ticks."

"Come on – sand is a lot more romantic than ticks, right? Give me some credit. I'm trying to get you out of your clothes in a clever way."

"I know," I said shyly. He hung his shorts over the tub railing, and I unhooked my bra under my shirt, pulled it off through my sleeve, shook it out, and said, "Okay. Sand free."

"That's it? That's all I get, a little peek of the outline of your nipples?" he asked. I shrugged my shoulders in such a way that indicated it wasn't all he would get; he walked over to me, pulled my shirt overhead, kissed me, and followed me into the bedroom.

For a moment, I felt beautiful as he ran his hands from my sides to up under my breasts and back down to unhook my shorts. I no longer felt the sting of sand between my thighs but felt waves of the kind of desire that usually precedes pain rushing through me. We were on the bed, and his hair hung loose above me, and his sand-stained feet pressed into mine, and his kisses tasted like the sea. I looked at him and said, "I like you so much," and then it all stopped.

"I'm sorry," he said and sat up abruptly. "I just don't think I can do this. I thought I could. I really did, but I can't."

I sat up too and said, "Are you just not ready for a relationship yet? Do you still have feelings for Holly?" I knew that wasn't it but thought I'd give him the easy out and let him use the line.

"No, it's not that," he said.

"Are you just not attracted to me?" I asked and covered my legs with the sheet.

"Yeah, I guess that's it," he said. "I thought I could do this, but I guess I can't. I'm just not used to this. I usually date girls with perfect bodies." I pulled the sheet up over my breasts and just sat there stunned. I couldn't understand why he'd told the truth. We weren't in a court room. He wasn't under oath, and my body wasn't on trial.

And the worst part of it was that I still had to get up and retrieve my clothes, had to display my defective body to Jude one more time before he left, but I did it. I pulled that sheet back down, stood up, slipped my shorts back over my thighs and walked back to the bathroom, breasts and stomach and back exposed, to get my t-shirt.

*

After Jude left that night, I took off all my clothes and stood in front of the full-length mirror on the back of my bedroom door. I looked over my shoulder at my back, noticed the way my thick thighs rubbed against each other, and stared at the places where my skin folded over itself a little just above my hips.

I didn't have the body of a model or an actress or someone an artist would wish to draw, but suddenly I didn't mind. The contrast between what Jude said and what I saw in the mirror that night somehow made me feel beautiful, made me feel strong.

I put on the black lace underwear that had been hiding at the back of the drawer since right after my honeymoon and slipped a delicate peach colored sheer chemise over my head. I studied the way the fabric collected around my breasts and stared into the sky and cloud colored flecks around the pupils of my eyes, and I knew that I could wait patiently for a man who would stay long enough to see the beautiful version of myself that I saw.

Chapter Thirteen: Home

It was August again in Beaumont, the month of greatest misery, the month when the old AC unit in my apartment struggled to keep the place below 85, the month when sweat soaked sheets painted a permanent stain of my figure on the mattress, the month when cool baths and memories of winter were the only things that sustained me. I was off for the summer and more than ready for my vacation to Minnesota the following week.

"What are you doing?" Abby asked.

"What kind of phone greeting is that?"

"Sorry. I was just trying to skip all the hello stuff," she said.

"You're so busy you can't even say hello?"

"No, I just thought we could get right into it this time."

"But it takes one second to say hello, maybe less than that," I said and watched as the second hand ticked across the curve of my wall clock.

"And now we've completely killed the point of skipping it," she said and sighed into the phone.

"Sorry. I'm literally lying naked on my linoleum kitchen floor. It's so hot in here, and it's the only thing that feels good right now. I guess we could say I've hit a low point."

"Wow."

"Yeah."

"Good thing you're coming to see me next week. It's 78 degrees here," she said. "We've officially reached the part of the year where my weather is better than yours."

"Oh, we've been there for about six months now."

*

Abby's apartment stood at the edge of Benson, a little town of less than 5,000 people out on the prairie in Western Minnesota. It was, like mine, one of those nondescript apartment buildings with beige-walled hallways, dark wood doors, and light brown carpet that stained far too easily, the kind of place where you lived before you got the place you really wanted to be. Still, she managed to create the illusion of permanence in the place by hanging dozens of framed photos, using pink-shaded lamps instead of the florescent overhead lights, and placing Persian rugs over huge patches of dull carpet.

"Wow. This looks like a real place," I said.

"What do you mean?"

"I mean it looks like an adult lives here. The last time I was here you still had that bean bag couch."

"I know. I finally got rid of all that old crap. It's like my mom always says, it's not good to take the poverty-motivated decorating choices of your twenties with you into your thirties. And, to be honest, it was getting harder and harder to get up out of that thing."

"I remember. I always had to do that awkward side-roll to get out of it."

"Yeah, it was awful. Just trust me. Spend a little more money than you think you should and get some new stuff, like I've been telling you – you need to get rid of those plastic dressers and buy some real furniture," she said.

"I have real furniture. It's not like I'm sitting on a blow-up couch or eating at a plastic picnic table."

"Don't you still have that card table?"

"So?"

"So your butt should be on a wooden chair and your underwear in a wooden drawer by the time you're thirty," she said.

"What's so great about wood? Why has wood been chosen as the material of adulthood?" I asked as we sat down at her new oak table.

*

After a night of pizza and movies, Abby was exhausted, but I couldn't sleep. Instead I sat silently on the floral bedspread in the spare room of her apartment and listened to the calm hum of the bugs outside the window. Back in Beaumont, overnight lows hovered around eighty, but in Benson the summer temperatures sometimes sunk as low as sixty. I felt the coolness of the window and suddenly couldn't stand to be inside. I searched my suitcase for the sweatshirt I hadn't worn in months, pulled it overhead, and headed for the door. I slipped on my shoes, quietly turned the lock, and snuck out of the apartment like a teenager heading into the excitement of the night.

Outside of the building, the dark country highway stretched out before me, barely illuminated by the full moon above and porch lamps from the occasional farmhouse. I walked quickly, following the white line on the edge of the lane, moving to the tall grass when a car passed by. I wasn't sure where I was going, but I wanted to get away from that floral bedspread, away from the apartment building, away from town and all the sleeping strangers who lived there.

I listened to the sound of my shoes on the pavement, the rhythmic thump of my specific stride. I felt the sweat bead against my back under the thick fabric of my sweatshirt, touched the skin, and tasted the salt on my fingers. I watched the shadowed swaying of midnight corn stalks, knowing next month they would be picked and plowed under, leaving the landscape a sea of dead stubs. I moved quicker and quicker, past the long gravel driveways to houses I couldn't see, quicker and quicker until I was running, racing against nothing, out into the desolate darkness of the night.

And then I stopped, stood alone on the empty highway, breathed in the cool Minnesota air, stared ahead for a moment at the road toward deeper darkness, but then headed back toward the glow of lights from town.

*

"Wake up," I half yelled at Abby as I shook the mattress beneath her.

"What happened? What's wrong?" she yelled while shaking herself awake by sitting up so fast she hit the back of her head against the wall.

"I figured it out."

"What? What time is it? Why are you dressed? What happened?"

"I went for a walk."

"You what?" she said, squinted in the direction of the alarm clock, and said, "It's 1:17. You left the apartment? Did you lock the door?"

"This might literally be the safest place on earth, and I didn't want to have to wake you up when I got back," I said.

"You *did* wake me up when you got back."

"Sorry."

"So what's going on? And this better be good."

"I'm sorry. I've just been going over this in my head, over and over again for years, and tonight I finally figured it out. I know why I married Blake."

"Why are you even thinking about him? Just let it go. Move on," she said and started to lie back down.

"That's the whole point. I had to figure it out before I could move on."

"Okay. It's one in the morning. You woke me up six hours before I have to get up for work. I'm listening. What's up?"

"The only reason I married him is because I didn't want to be by myself."

"That's the big revelation, that you didn't want to be by yourself? That's why everybody gets married."

"No, it's more than that. I didn't ever want to be by myself. I didn't even want to learn how. It's why I've spent the last three years trying to date everyone in Beaumont. It's not because I'm trying to fall in love. It's not even about that. I just don't want to sleep alone. I mean, how pathetic is that? I think I'd rather marry someone I'm just mediocre about than sit in a room alone, and so then what's left? What do I have then? So there's an idea of something sleeping next to me? Is that worth it? I mean, think about it, I had that whole relationship with Gary in college. It took me six months to figure out I hated that guy. I remember sitting on his futon in that stupid studio apartment watching him shave his face and realizing the only reason I was there was to avoid sleeping alone."

"I know. I remember."

"But it's worse than that. I was walking by myself tonight and –"

"Such a bad choice, by the way," she said.

"I know, but I had to. That's what I realized. I'm never alone … even my apartment isn't really like being alone. I can hear all the other people. It's like they're there with me, like I thought I needed that, and then tonight I was about as alone as a person can be, out on that road in the middle of the night, and I was fine. I had to see that – to really see that I could stand somewhere so alone and be just fine. I was out there looking at everything, at how beautiful it is here, and I suddenly realized I haven't been paying attention to my life. Think about it, I was in Galveston with Jude. Galveston. The land of pelicans and waves and sand-castles, but I didn't look at any of it. I can tell you exactly what Jude was wearing that day. I can tell you how his hair looked when the wind blew on the ferry and the frustrated way his face looked every time he tried to smooth it down. Hell, I can even conjure up the way he smelled that day, kind of a mixture of coconut sunscreen and that musky cologne deodorant that costs more than the stuff you find at the grocery store. But I didn't see Galveston. I just saw him. And then there's Wuthering Heights Park."

"What about the park?" she asked with a voice that seemed more annoyed than curious.

"I didn't go back for months because I was so worried about running into a guy whose name I don't even remember. I avoided a place I love because of some guy who probably didn't even think about me and wouldn't care if he did run into me anyway. I just feel so stupid," I said.

"You're not stupid."

"I am. It's all so stupid. Look at me – I got my dream job. I'm teaching college full time, and I haven't been focused on that. I've just been looking at what's missing in my life instead of what's—"

"Stop. I'm way too tired for the glass-is-half-full speech," she said. "And besides, life is way more complicated than that."

"Trust me, I know, but I think I realized something at my parents' house the other day."

"What's that?"

"I think I actually miss Beaumont."

"Really?"

"Yeah, I got this email from a student signed up for my creative writing class in the fall. She wanted to know what the assigned books were so she could get started on the reading early, and I felt kind of excited thinking about going back."

"Really?"

"Yeah, I started thinking about new things I could do with the class this year, like I heard about this assignment where you cut pictures of people out of magazines, not model-looking people but people who look real, and students each get one picture and write a story where the person in the picture is a character. It's supposed to help feed their creativity to think about who this person might be. They could do that character sketch assignment

I always give them, but they'd be doing it with an actual visual representation of who this person is. It seems like a cool starting point."

"Man, your job is so different from mine," she said and yawned.

"I know, but the thing is, thinking about all this again has got me so excited about everything the way I was when I was applying for teaching jobs and the way I was the day I interviewed for the job in Beaumont, and it made me realize that I don't think I want to apply for other jobs right now."

"Really? I thought you wanted to try to move back up north."

"I know. I thought so too, but I'm not sure anymore. I'm starting to think that maybe I'm supposed to be there, that maybe Beaumont is like the guy you don't like at first, the one who seems a little obnoxious and wears bad clothes, but then you find yourself thinking about him more and more until you realize you might be starting to actually like him. I mean, Beaumont is kind of beautiful in a not obvious and a gritty kind of way." As I spoke, my mind made the drive from the Houston airport to Beaumont, traveling past tiny Texas towns along Highway 90. I could almost see the late afternoon ditches filled with egrets and the occasional beer bottle, the run-down roadside stands selling brisket and live crawfish, the old bridges over bayous, and the dilapidated diner that never recovered from the hurricane and still sat boarded up along the lonely stretch of highway out past the edge of Beaumont. I thought about how Beaumont didn't have an elaborate welcome sign, how the unadorned green population marker was good enough for them. I thought about how some slogan on an expensive sign couldn't possibly define what a city was anyhow. The only way to really know was to stay a while and study the place. "I can't believe I've been so focused on guys when I've been surrounded by so much poverty and so many people coping with real problems," I said. "I feel so stupid." I looked over at Abby's sleepy face.

"Come on – you're not the only person who's done stupid

things because of guys."

"That's easy for you to say. You could probably go three years without having a date and not even care that much," I said.

"Yeah, now, but that wasn't always the case."

"Yeah, right."

"Look, I'm really tired and kind of out of it right now, so I'm gonna tell you something I've never told anyone before," she said and slowly sat up.

"Okay."

She pulled her knees up toward her, stared straight at me, and said, "When I was in fourth grade this guy, Sam Schuller, was the cutest boy in class. Everybody liked him. On picture day I gave him one of the wallet sized pictures of me, and that was a really big deal. My parents always ordered the small package where you only get like five wallets. I remember it vividly to this day. He took the picture, looked at it, looked at me, laughed, tore it in half, let it fall to the floor, and walked away." She said this with a pain in her eyes I hadn't seen before.

"That's horrible."

"I know, right? And so, from that day on, I hated that guy, I mean, like really hated that guy. Over the years, I built it up in my head more and more, devising plan after plan, first of ways to humiliate him and later thinking of ways to rise above him. I somehow got it into my head that being a lawyer was the height of success in life. I had this idea that if I could just become a lawyer and run into Sam Schuller and tell him how important I was, that all would be right with the world."

"So that's why you went to law school?" I asked.

"No ... I don't think so. I think by that point it was less about him and more about me, but that's where it started. That's what put the idea in my head."

"Gotcha."

"But that's not the point of the story," she said.

"So what's the point of the story?"

"So a couple of years ago I'm at my ten year high school reunion, and there he is – Sam Schuller – and he's not cute anymore. He's put on a lot of weight, and he's wearing the kind of clothes that only accentuate the lumpiness of his body, and so all night I avoid talking to him. I just sit there, still hating this guy, and then the drinks come, and I drink way too much. Eventually I notice that he's about to leave, and I feel the old rage coming back. I run up to him, and I say, 'Hi, Sam Schuller,' and he says, 'Hey, Abby,' and I say, '*Hey, Abby? Hey, Abby?* That's all you have to say to me? I would just like you to know that even though you ripped up my picture, I became a lawyer.' He looks at me and says, 'What picture?' and then I just stand there for a moment feeling stupid before I rush out of the high school gym to my car."

"Wow. So he didn't even remember?"

"Of course not. It was fourth grade."

"And it never occurred to you that the massive grudge you were holding was not even on his radar?"

"No, it never did, but that's not my point," she said.

"What's your point?"

"The point is I became a lawyer, and I don't know if I would've done that if stupid Sam Schuller hadn't ripped up my picture in fourth grade. What I'm trying to say is yes, maybe sometimes you are too focused on guys, but maybe that's not all bad. Maybe that's just the thing that gets you to where you need to be. I mean, think about it. You married Blake. That put you in a situation where you were with a guy who didn't really want a future. He didn't want kids. He didn't really want to settle down. He stalled those parts of your life."

"And how is that a good thing?" I asked.

"Because you finished graduate school. You got a job teaching at a university. Maybe being stalled from some things is what gave you the other things."

"Wow. You're smart when you're groggy. I should wake you up in the middle of the night more often."

"Please don't," she said and pulled the pink quilt back up over her knees.

"Can I sleep in here tonight? You have a queen. I won't even get close to you."

"I don't know. I'm worried I'm gonna wake up to you cuddling me like Sara did that time in college."

"No, I promise. I'll stay on my side."

"So after your grand declaration about how you have a hard time being alone you want to sleep here so you're not alone?" she said and laughed.

"I know, but you're not a guy. That's progress, right?" I said and slipped under the blanket.

"I guess so, and I'm too tired to care right now," she said and flipped off the light.

*

The following week I sat by myself in an airplane headed back to Texas. The people around me chatted with their companions, raced through pages of interesting novels, settled in under fleece blankets to sleep away the flight, and subtly nodded along to the music playing on their headphones. I opened the shade and peered out the small passenger window as we ascended further and further up. It was a rainy day in Minneapolis, giving the atmosphere the kind of muted presence that painters achieve by adding gray tones where color once was. I watched as we passed over dozens of lakes and neighborhoods I once knew, up over the skyscrapers of Minneapolis and the highways and bridges and tiny cars below. Up and up we went, closer and closer to the clouds that covered the city below, and then there we were for a moment – right in the middle of a cloud, nothing but gray beyond my window. But we kept ascending, and suddenly we were above it all, and there was the sun, and I thought about how life is like that. Sometimes you're in the middle of a rainstorm, but there's something you can't see on the other side.

"Oh, my God," I accidentally said aloud.

"It's okay, dear," the older woman sitting next to me said and grabbed my arm.

"Oh, no. I'm not afraid of flying. I'm just –"

"It's okay. There's nothing to be afraid of. It'll get a lot less bumpy when we reach our cruising altitude," she said with a smile on her weathered face.

And she was right. There really was nothing to be afraid of. Somewhere miles and miles ahead and far below was Beaumont, Texas. I didn't know what I would find when I got there, but I was going home.

CPSIA information can be obtained
at www.ICGtesting.com
Printed in the USA
FFOW04n1742170617
36751FF